LAST SEEN WEARING TRAINERS

ROSIE RUSHTON

LAST SEEN WEARING TRAINERS

Andersen Press • London

First published in 2002 by
Andersen Press Limited,
20 Vauxhall Bridge Road, London SW1V 2SA
www.andersenpress.co.uk

© 2002 by Rosie Rushton

The right of Rosie Rushton to be identified as the author of
this work has been asserted by her in accordance with the
Copyright, Designs and Patents Act, 1988.

British Library Cataloguing in Publication Data available
ISBN 1 84270 065 0

Typeset by FiSH Books, London WC1
Printed and bound in Great Britain by Mackays of Chatham Ltd., Chatham, Kent

For everyone who has been scared by someone they love; and for all those with the courage to face their fears

KATIE
Thursday June 28th
7.30 p.m.

I can't believe I'm actually going to go. I never thought I would. Oh, we talked about it a lot, Joe and I; he's been dead keen for weeks now, but I've always chickened out at the last moment – told myself that things weren't really that bad. But that was before last weekend. Last weekend changed everything.

Not that things haven't been changing for what seems like forever. It started when Dad died. No, that's not true. It started long before that, I guess; maybe as far back as when my brother Tom was just a toddler. It's simply that at the time, I didn't realise what was happening. You don't when you're just a kid; you get told that your mum's got a headache because you've been naughty, and you believe it. You get smacked and you really believe it when she says you need some sense knocking into you. You catch your dad crying in the greenhouse, but when he says he's got something in his eye, you go along with it. You want to, so you do.

And if someone tells you that you are totally useless, you believe that too. I would still be believing it if it wasn't for Joe.

I met Joe a couple of weeks after we moved into the village. It was going to be another of Mum's fresh starts, leaving the town and coming to Hartfield.

'You see, Pumpkin,' she said (she calls me Pumpkin when she has a good day), 'you see, it'll make all the difference being in the country, in a nice little community. We won't know ourselves.'

I didn't want to come. For one thing, I wasn't convinced that anything we did would make a difference, and for another I was fed up with moving house. We came up to Kettleborough from Sussex after Mum's first 'little bit of trouble' as Dad called it. Then, after the business with the neighbours opposite, we moved to a new estate on the other side of town. Things got worse while we were there; it's hard to hide on an estate, and people started talking – Mum never closed the windows before she yelled – and kids at school sneered at me and said that their parents thought we were a dead weird lot.

We were.

You couldn't fault them for accuracy.

Then eighteen months ago, Dad went and – well, he died.

It was in the papers and everything. There was even a bit on 'Look East Today' on the television.

It was awful. People say they understand what you are going through, but they don't. Not really. How can they, when their lives carry on just the same as usual? I used to wake up at night and see his face on the ceiling; I used to imagine that I heard his voice on the stairs. I would burst into tears at all the wrong times and once I had started to cry, I couldn't stop.

It was horrible.

But the anger was worse. Is worse.

I get so mad at Dad for leaving us. Leaving me, really. Because it's me who has to pick up the pieces; me who has to cope with Mum when she has her black moods, me who takes the flak for everything that goes wrong. Dad used to sort it – or at least try to. Now there's no one except me. He shouldn't have gone and died. It wasn't fair.

I was devastated for weeks after Dad died, but funnily enough, once the funeral was over, Mum seemed to perk up a bit. I thought she'd be worse than ever, but she wasn't. She got a new hairdo and started wearing make-up again.

She began cooking meals instead of buying them frozen at the supermarket and she even talked about getting a part-time job.

'You've got to admire her bravery,' Grace, Mum's best friend, used to murmur to anyone who would listen.

'You must be very proud of your mum,' the teachers at school would say to me practically every day.

'Life has sent her some hard knocks, you can't deny it,' my gran wrote in a letter from Scotland where she was keeping well out of the way.

I wanted to write back and tell her that when it came to hard knocks, Mum was pretty good at dishing them out as well. But I didn't.

You don't want people to know. It's easier to let them think that the mother they see out in the street is the one you live with behind closed doors.

So I just carried on, lurching from day to day, hoping that the good patch would last forever. I tried really hard to be good and stay quiet, and not drive her to drink.

It didn't work for very long.

It never does.

A few weeks after Dad's funeral, we had this awful row. I can't even remember what it was about now, but I said something that she didn't like and she went ballistic.

'You'll be the death of me!' she screeched, pulling at her hair the way she does when she's going into one of her mood crashes. 'You and your ways. I don't know what I ever did to deserve a kid like you. Trouble from the very start, that's what you've been!'

'Well, I never wanted to be born!' I yelled back, the first time she said it to me. 'And certainly not to a cow like you!'

That was when she pushed me downstairs. She didn't mean to, of course – she just lashed out and my foot slipped and that was that. An accident, really. My fault for being

3

lippy. Especially when she was having a bad day. I should have had more sense.

We didn't tell them the truth in Casualty. Mum said I'd fallen off my bike and I knew better than to put them right. I did get the feeling that the doctor was about to ask a lot of questions but Tom had one of his screaming fits and I think after that they were just thankful to plaster my arm and get rid of us.

We took a taxi home, I remember, and Mum cuddled me and kissed the top of my head and cried a lot and said she was so sorry for everything, but I did see that God had sent her just too much to bear and it wasn't her fault if she snapped every now and again, was it?

She promised that from now on things were going to be different and I believed her. Like I said, you believe what you want to believe, and to be fair, she was really nice for quite a while after that. Even Tom noticed it; Tom doesn't say much but you can tell how he's feeling because he stops his rocking and finger tapping and hums a lot and does his drawing.

He's OK, Tom. Just different from other kids. But OK.

Anyway, it was shortly after this that Mum decided to move to Hartfield. It's only five miles from Kettleborough, but really quiet and countrified. I think she chose Hartfield because Grace lives here and she and Grace have been friends for years and years. Grace is ten years older than Mum and really nice. Not clever or witty or anything, but safe and comfortable and always the same. I like that in a person.

There are lots of thatched cottages in the village – not that we got one of those, just a dilapidated semi at the bottom of Church Hill. It was all Mum could afford and she wouldn't have been able to buy that if my gran – Dad's mother – hadn't died six months earlier and left her some money.

I didn't want to move, but Mum seemed so upbeat about it and even sang round the house a few times and I thought that

4

if it meant things being normal, I'd do anything. It wasn't even as if I would have to leave my school; Pipers Court takes people from miles around and it just meant a longer bus ride and more time to daydream.

So I kept quiet and we came here.

It hasn't made her happy though – nothing much does in the long run, except brandy and old black and white movies.

Don't get me wrong – it's not her fault. I mean, those neighbours back in Kettleborough used to mutter behind their hands and say she was a disgrace and ought to pull her socks up and get on with life, but then, what did they know? They didn't know about Mum being brought up in a kids' home and then getting pregnant and having a baby that died at three months, did they? Or about – well, all the other things that happened, and how people always blamed Mum when really it wasn't down to her.

That's why she's in a mess – because of the past and all that. She's told me that a zillion times and most of the time, I believe her. Only sometimes, I just wish she could forget the past and get on with living in the present. She says she does try and I guess in her own way she does.

Anyway, we had only been in the new house a couple of weeks when I met Joe. It was the first time that I skived off school. Mum had had a real go at me that morning, shouted, slapped me, called me names, the works. Thankfully, the minibus had already called to take Tom to Lime Lodge – that's his special school; he gets dead upset when Mum shouts at me and it sets him back for days. Funny – she never yells directly at him, not even when he throws his food or screams or bangs his head on the wall. It's as if, because he can't argue back, she can be really patient with him. It's odd.

That morning, I didn't even bother yelling back at her – I just ran out of the house and kept on running. I wasn't even aware of where I was going; my eyes were blurred with tears and the only thing I could think about was getting as far away from her as possible. I didn't even care that it was raining and all I had on was my school skirt and sweater. I was angry; not just with her, not just with Dad, but with myself. Angry that I had been dumb enough to believe that things might get better, angry that, even though I was fourteen, I still let it happen, over and over again.

And angry because, try as I might, I couldn't think of any way that I could stop it happening.

I should have caught the bus to school but I didn't. By the time I heard it coming, I was out of the village and on the road to Frampton. It was raining steadily by then, and I dodged behind some bushes in Spectacle Lane and watched the bus rumble past. I could see Alice peering out of the window, rubbing away the condensation with one hand, her face all screwed-up and anxious. Alice is my best mate and the one person I've often been tempted to tell the whole truth to. But she's really sassy and clued up and I know she would have told me to do something about it, and not just sit there and take it. Or worse, she would have marched over to my house and had it out with Mum.

And that wouldn't have helped me at all.

Now at last I *am* going to do something about it, and I can't tell her. Joe was really firm about that, and I know he's right.

'We're doing this for you, Katie,' he said last night, stroking my hair the way he does when I get upset. 'And if it's going to work, then it has to be our secret. You do see that, don't you?'

I do. Of course I do.

But it would be nice to tell Alice, because then she could keep an eye on Tom.

I worry about Tom. He's only ten and what with his learning difficulties and the fact that he can't put things into words, he doesn't have friends like most kids his age. There's just me and Mum – oh, and Grace, of course, who watches him if Mum's out.

6

I can't tell Grace what I'm planning.

I can't tell anyone.

I told Joe that I worried about my brother but he was really sensible and said that Tom was not my problem, and that everyone had to sort their own lives out before they could be strong enough to help others.

He sees things so much more clearly than I do.

That's one of the reasons I love him.

I didn't love him straight away. I don't want you to think that I just saw him that day and went all starry-eyed and gooey; it wasn't like that.

I was behind the bushes, watching the bus disappear and suddenly, in my head, there was Dad's voice.

'The wheels on the bus go round and round, round and round, round and round!'

He used to sing that to me when I was little.

'The wheels on the bus go round and round, all day long!'

It was as if Dad was there, behind the tree beside me. I could almost smell his sandalwood aftershave, practically feel the touch of his hand on my cheek.

For just the briefest moment, I felt his arms going round me, pulling me towards him in one of those big bear hugs that squeeze the breath out of you – and then there was nothing. Just the breeze blowing the leaves and the sound of the bus disappearing round the bend onto the main road.

I don't know how long I stood there, crying and shouting and hammering my fists on the tree trunk. It sounds crazy now, but the rain had eased and there was no one around, just a few sheep in the field behind. I yelled at Dad for dying and at Mum for not being like she used to be and I even yelled at Tom for being able to live in that world inside his head and switch off from all the things he doesn't want to know about.

Most of all, I yelled at myself.

'Why do you do it, you stupid, useless cow?' I sobbed,

thumping my balled fist against the side of my head. 'Why do you make her so angry? Why can't you just be quiet and keep out of her way? You're pathetic. Pathetic! PATHETIC!'

I hadn't heard the van coming up the lane. I didn't even hear it pull up. It was the banging of the driver's door that made me jump.

'Can I help?'

I spun round, rubbing the back of my hand across my running nose. A sandy-haired guy in a dark blue sweater and jeans was peering anxiously at me.

'No, I'm fine!' I stammered.

All those warnings about talking to strangers rushed through my head and I realised with a sinking feeling that I had left my personal alarm on the hall table. You see, Mum does love me a lot really; she got me the alarm when we moved, because she said you never knew what strange types you might meet out in the countryside. She wouldn't have done that if she hadn't loved me, deep down.

The guy smiled and flicked a stray strand of hair from his eye. He couldn't have been more than nineteen, and he didn't look like a raving psychopath. In fact, he looked pretty fit from where I was standing. But I wasn't taking any chances.

'I don't think you're fine at all,' he said as I began walking purposefully away from him down the lane. 'Can I phone someone?'

'What?'

I paused and looked at him. He had really high cheekbones, and his voice was deep and throaty, like an actor's; the sort of voice Alice would say was dead sexy. That's another thing Alice is clued up about: men.

'Well,' he said, 'I'm not about to offer you a lift – for all you know I could be a convict on the run!'

He turned and pulled open the door of the van. That was when I noticed the poppies. There was one painted on the door and one huge one over the roof, its bright green leaves surroundings the windows. And there was a ladybird daubed on one of the wheel arches and a spider climbing over the bumper. Really arty.

The guy grabbed a mobile phone from the pocket of a waterproof jacket hanging over the seat.

'Maybe I could call someone? You look like you are in some sort of trouble.'

I shook my head.

'No, honestly,' I said. 'I'm OK. I just had a row with – with someone, but I'm fine now.'

'Boyfriend?' he asked.

I shook my head.

'Mum,' I muttered, and then wondered why on earth I should be standing on the edge of the road talking to a perfect stranger.

'Ah,' he said knowingly. 'Mothers.'

He took a deep breath and let it out slowly as if considering what to say next.

'So you bunked off school, right?' he remarked, opening the van door and flinging the mobile phone onto the seat.

I shrugged. For all I knew, he could be one of those plain clothes police guys that they've started having on the streets in Kettleborough, checking up on kids who play truant.

'I used to do that when things got tough,' he said conversationally. 'You just can't face all your mates chatting on about music and discos and the latest football scores while your world is falling apart.'

'That's just it!' I heard myself exclaim, even before the words had formed in my head. 'They just don't know they are born, some of them. That is ... I mean ... '

I was beginning to wish I had kept quiet, but he appeared not to notice my hesitation.

'You just want to be alone to sort out your head,' he

continued. 'And I guess the one thing you don't want is some inquisitive guy in a clapped-out van giving you the third degree at the roadside!'

He grinned apologetically and I couldn't help smiling back. That's when I noticed his eyes – one was greeny blue and the other was grey. I've got odd coloured eyes too; kids at primary school used to tease me about them. And in nearly fifteen years I've never met anyone else whose eyes didn't match.

'I'm Joe, by the way,' he said. 'And you are?'

'Katie,' I said. 'Katie Fordyce.'

'Katie.' He murmured my name, nodded and then, smiling, he stretched out a hand.

'Glad to know you, Katie,' he said. 'So! How about I give you a lift to your school?'

'No thanks!' I replied hastily and turned to go.

He clapped his hand to his forehead.

'What a dumb thing to say!' he sighed. 'Of course, you're quite right. Like I said, you would be mad to accept a lift from a stranger. There again,' he added, looking up at the sky where great banks of grey clouds were gathering over Coopers Hill, 'it looks as if there is more rain on the way and you're already soaked to the skin. How far have you got to go?'

'Pipers Court,' I said hastily, even though I had no intention of going to school. 'There'll be another bus soon.'

It wasn't true. That's one of the downsides of living in a village; you wait for hours between buses and there's never one around when you most need it.

'I doubt it,' he said calmly. 'Look, I've got an idea.'

He reached into the van, picked up his mobile phone and thrust it into my hands.

'Take that, and climb in!' he suggested. 'If I don't drive you straight to school, and behave in the most proper manner you could imagine, you can phone for help and have me arrested!'

He looked so earnest that I couldn't help laughing.

'OK, thanks,' I said. 'Cool van.'

He nodded.

'I like to be different,' he grinned. 'It's amazing what you can do with a pot of paint and a bit of imagination. Now, which way is school?'

'I don't want to go to school.'

'Home?' he suggested, raising one eyebrow as I climbed into the van.

Of course, that was out of the question. If Mum thought I'd skived off school I'd be asking for a real bashing.

I bit my lip.

'Seat belt,' ordered Joe, turning the key in the ignition.

I clunked the belt into place as the van lurched forward.

'I'll be for it if I turn up at school late – and I'll be for it if I don't,' I sighed.

'The way I see it is this,' continued Joe, glancing over his shoulder as he pulled out into the lane. 'Whatever you decide, you have to be in charge. You have to get to them before they get to you.'

'Pardon?'

'Well, let's say you decide to go to school,' he explained. 'When you get there, you march up to the office, or Reception or whatever it is, and you look them straight in the eye.'

'Oh sure!' I said sarcastically. 'And they'll tell me it's lovely to see me and all will be hunky-dory. Not!'

He laughed.

'All you have to do is say that you are dreadfully sorry you are late, but your mum's car broke down and you had to walk the rest of the way...'

'Mum doesn't drive,' I interjected

'OK,' he said, slowing down as he approached the crossroads. 'So how about this? You missed the bus, a guy offered you a lift, but you have listened so carefully to all the lectures about strange men, that you simply had to refuse and walk to school instead. And that's why you are late!'

He threw back his head and roared with laughter at his own inventiveness.

Maybe that was when I fell in love with him.

Certainly that was when bits of me that have never tingled before began to make their presence felt.

'All right,' I said. 'I'll give it a go.'

'Great,' Joe grinned. 'So where do I go?'

'Oh, sorry,' I said. 'Turn left here, then right onto the dual carriageway and it's the second exit. About four miles, I'm afraid. Don't you live round here then?'

Joe shook his head.

'I come over this way once a week for this and that,' he said. 'Checking things out.'

'So are you at college?' I asked. 'Or working?'

He laughed and rammed the van into top gear.

'I'm studying life!' he grinned, 'and trying to work out just what I want to do with mine. What about you? I mean, what are you going to do with yours?'

Well, from then until we got close to my school, we talked about everything. No, that's silly; of course we didn't. I didn't talk about Mum or Dad or Tom or what it was like to be me. And he didn't tell me anything about his family or friends. Not then. Instead, we talked about fate and destiny and the meaning of life. I'd never thought about some of the things that Joe said – like how we are all on a long walk through life and we have to read the signposts and follow the clues along the way, if we're going to get where destiny intends us to be. How we have to do things, not let things be done to us. There was a whole lot more stuff like that, and to be honest I didn't understand everything he was going on about, but that didn't matter because just listening to the sound of his voice was enough.

'You'd better stop here!' I exclaimed as we turned off the dual carriageway into Mortimer Road. 'That's my school, at the top of the hill.'

Joe pulled up at the side of the road.

'Now remember,' he said. 'Look them straight in the eye and don't let them put you down. OK?'

'OK!' I agreed.

And then I said something really dumb. Alice would have gone ballistic and told me I was totally uncool.

'Will I see you again?'

Joe looked straight into my eyes.

'That,' he said, 'depends.'

'On what?' I whispered.

'On fate, on destiny,' he said.

Then he leaned forward, so close to me that I could feel his breath on my neck.

'And on you.'

With that, he threw the van into gear and shot off up the hill, his tyres throwing up dust as he sped away.

I walked slowly up to school feeling strangely elated. It was as if I had been living inside a windowless box for a very long time and then, suddenly, someone had come along and cut a slit in the cardboard. Only a tiny slit, but enough for me to see that there was something worth looking at outside.

And that, just possibly, I might be able to reach it.

So that's how it all started. That's how I come, a year later, aged exactly fifteen and a half today, to be sitting on the end of my bed, in my unusually tidy bedroom, with my rucksack hidden at the back of my wardrobe, stashed full of new clothes.

The clothes were Joe's idea too, and he bought most of them for me. He even bought me a bottle of really cool perfume – *Beginnings*, it's called, because he said this was going to be the beginning of a new life for me. He's so thoughtful. I nearly landed myself in it over the perfume though. I was so thrilled when he gave it to me last week, that I splashed it all over me on the way home, and of course Mum smelt it at once.

'What are you wearing?' she demanded. 'I hope you didn't go spending your clothes allowance on a load of trashy scent!'

I told her that I'd been to Alice's house and she'd squirted me with her freebie perfume from *Heaven Sent* magazine, and she seemed to believe me. She went on a bit about it making me smell like a slag and how if she ever caught me spending money on cheap stuff like that, she'd have my guts for garters – but what's new? At least she never discovered the bag of new clothes that Joe had given me.

I didn't want him to spend money on clothes, but he said that if I wore stuff I already had Mum would be able to tell the police what was missing and they might catch up with us before we had a chance to get very far.

I got a bit scared when he talked about the police but he told me not to worry. We're coming back after a week or so – or maybe two. It's all being done to give Mum a fright; to make her see that she can't treat me like she did last weekend. OK, so she didn't mean it, but she has to see a doctor and get some pills or something. She scares me.

I don't want to think about last weekend now, though. It makes me feel sick.

Mum will be back in a minute. She's been to my Parents' Evening, so heaven knows what kind of mood she'll be in. It never used to be a problem but lately the teachers have been going on at me about falling grades and lack of concentration, and I guess they'll tell Mum. Thankfully, Grace is downstairs, keeping an eye on Tom and watching 'EastEnders'. When Mum gets in they'll sit down and have a drink together. Hopefully, Mum will have two or three and be all soft and soppy for a bit, before the nastiness sets in. That's when I'll tell her about tomorrow – not the truth, of course, but my brilliant alibi.

And by the time she finds out that it's all lies, I'll be miles away with Joe and she won't have a clue where I am.

Serve her right.

I do hope she'll miss me.

LYDIA
Thursday June 28th
8.15 p.m.

My feet are killing me. What an evening! I don't know why I bothered going. These Parents' Evenings don't do you any good. Well, not when you've got a kid like Katie. With Tom, it's different; people don't expect much of Tom and when he manages to do something new, or eats his dinner nicely, the teachers are really thrilled and they tell you it's all down to you for being such a good mum with him.

It's not like that with Katie. Oh no. Katie's always been as bright as a button, really clever. I don't know who she gets it from – certainly not her father. Of course, I'm not stupid; don't go thinking that. But I've had a hard life and never been able to make the most of my potential the way I might have done, had things been different. Not that I'm complaining. I've never been one to complain. People admire that in me.

The trouble with Katie is that she doesn't realise how lucky she is. If I'd had the chances she's getting, there's no telling what I might have done. It's not just any school, Pipers Court; it's always high up in those league tables they publish and if I had to pay the fees, she wouldn't be there, I can tell you. But when Jarvis died, I discovered he'd paid a lump sum to cover the fees till Katie was eighteen. I was furious, I can tell you. I didn't even know he had that kind of money – he was always wittering on about how we couldn't afford a holiday and why didn't I get a job. What with everything that happened, there were better things a sum like that could have been put to. Still, there was nothing I could do about it; I couldn't get the money back.

They've been very good, the teachers – I have to give them their due. Not a week passed after Jarvis died without one of them telephoning to ask if everything was all right, and to say that they were keeping a close eye on Katie, to make sure she was coping. I told them that they didn't have to worry: Katie was fine. It was me that was struggling, what with the strain of having Tom to deal with and the death of my darling Jarvis. I knew they were all impressed by my courage; but as I said to them, it doesn't do to give in. We all have our cross to bear. Wonderful, they said I was. Wonderful and so brave.

They all say that Katie's a good kid, but then they don't live with her. No, no, that's not fair. She's not a bad kid deep down and I love her. I do honestly. It's just that she's so strong willed and – well, a typical teenager, I guess. And she's been far too used to getting her own way. That's Jarvis's fault, of course. When I had my first bout of – well, being under the weather – he kept saying I had to get a grip on things, because Katie would get upset. It was as though her happiness was more important to him than mine. He'd always been sweet with her, but after Tom came along and they told us he would never be quite normal, it was as if Jarvis focused all his love and attention onto Katie. When she got a good report, he'd buy her all manner of things; when she won the drama cup at school, he arranged for the local paper to take her picture. I told him she would get spoiled, but he just laughed. I was right, of course. And who is it that has to deal with her now? Me. Everything is always left to me.

But I do hate myself when I lash out at her. I just see – well, HIM – and then I think of the awful way I treated . . . No, I mustn't let myself dwell. I'm doing very well. I'm a good woman really.

When I got to the school tonight, I was all set to be in and out in half an hour. I'd asked Grace to sit with Tom – Katie can't cope if he has one of his screaming fits – and I was

17

looking forward to getting back for a brandy and Coke and good old natter. But no sooner had I got inside the door, than it started. First it was Mrs Wainwright, Katie's year tutor, saying that her grades are dropping and she wondered whether everything was all right at home?

Absolutely hunky-dory, I wanted to say – if you forget about the dead husband and the mental – sorry, learning disadvantaged – son. But of course I didn't.

'We're soldiering on, Mrs Wainwright,' I replied with a gentle smile. 'I'll have a word with Katie. These teenagers – they just don't apply themselves, do they?'

Mrs Wainwright nodded and smiled at me. I suppose they don't get many helpful and understanding parents at these things.

'Of course,' she added, 'we must remember that Katie got a bit behind when she broke her arm falling off that bicycle.'

Well, I couldn't let myself think about that so I stood up and told her I would make sure Katie pulled her socks up. I told her I wouldn't take any nonsense from my daughter, and I could guarantee things would get better. She started making soothing noises about bereavement and allowing everyone time to readjust, but I just nodded and smiled and headed off to see Mr Stoker.

I quite like Mr Stoker – Barry, his name is; he's the kind of man you could get it together with if he wasn't already married and Katie's maths teacher.

'Ah, Mrs Fordyce, how lovely to see you again!' he said as I pulled up a chair to the table. 'Now, let me see – ah yes!'

He pulled out a folder marked KATIE FORDYCE – YEAR TEN and peered at it.

'I don't quite understand what is going on,' he murmured, pulling at the little goatee beard on his chin. 'Katie was doing so well last year – she had a really good grasp of all the basic principles, and I had high hopes.'

I didn't say anything. I could tell from his voice that the high hopes were fairly low now.

'But this year,' he said, sighing deeply. 'This year she's really lost her way.'

He looked up at me enquiringly. He really does have the most gorgeous eyes.

'Is there any reason for this?'

I dropped my eyes and bit my lip, leaving just the right pause for him to lean anxiously towards me.

'My husband's death – I know it's been a while now, but it hit all of us very hard.'

I put my hand to my forehead.

'My dear Mrs Fordyce, I do understand,' he nodded and for one moment I thought he was going to pat my hand. 'Don't you worry – I'm sure Katie will get back on track soon. Lovely girl; credit to you.'

I smiled, touched his hand ever so briefly, and moved on to Miss McAllister, who teaches History.

I haven't met her before – she was new last term. She didn't look old enough to be out of school, never mind teaching. She looked about eighteen, all ginger hair and freckles and one of those silly little cardigans with beads and bits of midriff sticking out.

'Ah,' she started. 'Mrs Fordyce – Katie's mum?'

I nodded.

She flicked through some papers.

'I have to confess to being a little worried about Katie,' she began, in a breathy little girl sort of voice. 'Perhaps you can help me.'

She looked up expectantly.

'I'll try,' I said.

'When I came here, I was told she was one of our brighter students.'

I nodded.

'Always has been,' I said. 'Mind you, I've always encouraged her – bought books and things, you know. Some parents – they just don't bother themselves, do they?'

Miss McAllister didn't seem to take much notice of that.

'To begin with, she seemed to be doing just fine,' she went on. 'But now...'

She sighed.

'Now, her work is handed in late, it's lacking in imagination, full of careless mistakes – and yet I know she has a very good brain. What is going on?'

Now I don't know why I said what I did – except that I'm into my menopause and believe me, there can't be many women who are going through what I have to suffer right now.

'Could it be that you are a bad teacher?' I asked. 'Katie's brainy, you said that. So it must be you.'

Miss McAllister went bright red – ginger-headed people always blush easily, I've found – and started coughing.

'I – I don't think it's that,' she murmured. 'I mean, I hope not.'

She swallowed hard.

'Is there anything worrying Katie? Any trouble at home? You must be very distressed following your husband's untimely death.'

'Oh yes,' I nodded. 'Distraught.'

I dabbed at my eye with a tissue but the woman just blundered on.

'Could it be that in your unhappiness you've failed to deal with Katie's emotional...'

Well, that did it.

'Oh I get it!' I said, banging my fists on the table. 'That's typical of you teachers, that is! A kid decides not to work hard, and it's all put down to the mother's fault. She loses interest in your subject and you immediately think that her entire home life is falling apart. You don't have a clue, do you?'

'Mrs Fordyce, please ... ' she began, but I wasn't having any of it.

'You sit there, hardly out of nappies yourself, spouting a load of psychological claptrap at someone old enough to be your mother! Are you married? No. Have you any kids? Of course not. But you are only too ready to tell me how to deal with my own daughter! You've got a bloody nerve! I've a good mind to ... '

I would probably have gone on for a lot longer, but I was suddenly aware that the room had gone very quiet. In fact, you could have heard a pin drop. I glanced sideways. Everyone was looking at me and out of the corner of my eye I could see Mrs Wainwright heading my way.

'Now, what seems to be the problem here?' she said, as the buzz of conversation started up around the room.

'The problem, Mrs Wainwright,' I said, 'is sitting behind this table.'

I gestured towards the now-scarlet Miss McAllister and then let my face soften into what I believe was an understanding smile.

'But please – don't be too harsh on her. She's young. She's new to teaching. And to life.'

I inclined my head in Miss McAllister's direction.

'Don't apologise, my dear,' I said holding up a hand. 'I've read all about classroom stress. Just let's forget you ever said those terrible things, shall we?'

Miss McAllister opened her mouth but I carried straight on.

'Oh yes, I know I could report you – but I won't. We all have to learn, don't we, dear? And now, if you will excuse me, I must get back to poor Tom. He's disabled, you know. It's not easy ... but there we are.'

I don't know what Mrs Wainwright said to Miss McAllister. I didn't stop to find out.

But I rather think she will have had the last word.

So it's no wonder I'm worn out. Still, I was lucky that a bus came just as I crossed the main road outside the school. I'll be back home within twenty minutes with a stiff drink in my hand. By golly, I need it.

Of course, if Jarvis were here, I'd get the lecture about alcohol not being the answer to life's problems. The way he used to go on, you would think I was a raving alcoholic. He never understood that a little tot of brandy helped to stop the shakes. There's a lot Jarvis never understood.

But he's not here. Mind you, there are times when I fancy he's standing right beside me, whispering softly.

'Lyddy, Lyddy, calm down!' That's what he used to say when I had one of my turns. Sometimes when Katie drives me crazy or I start losing control, I can almost feel his hand on my shoulder, pushing me gently into the nearest chair. Of course, I know it's not him – I may be on tranquillisers but I'm not crazy. Still, it gives me the shivers.

I shall be glad to get home. I bet Katie's gone to bed. Probably thinks that by pretending to be asleep, she'll escape the lecture that's coming. Well, she's got another think coming.

Still, I need that drink first.

Katie can wait.

TOM
Thursday June 28th
8.35 p.m.

Something odd is happening. I know it is.

Something's different.

But what?

The house smells the same. Sometimes when things change, the smells change too, like when they took Dad away with a cloth over him. People kept coming and bringing flowers so that the whole house smelt like the garden in the park where they used to put me in my buggy while Katie went on the swings.

There aren't any visitors to make it feel different. Just Grace who lives in the house with the blue front door – and she doesn't count. Grace is OK. She doesn't rush about like other people and she doesn't come up behind me and make me jump. Apart from Grace, I don't much like visitors. Sometimes people come to the house to see Mum and they don't look at me. They look past me and won't talk to me. That makes me really angry. I shout at them and wave my hands to try to make them see me, but it never makes any difference. They just pick up their handbags and say they really have to go, or else they disappear into the kitchen with Mum and never stop to find out what I want. Stupid, stupid people.

I know one thing that's different. Katie's in her bedroom. She shouldn't be, not now. She does her homework up there but then she comes downstairs and watches TV or talks to me and looks at my drawing. I'm good at drawing. I may not be good at very much but my drawing is ace. That's a new word: ace. I like it. Katie taught it to me. It means really, really good; the best. Katie said so.

Why hasn't Katie come down? Something's happening and I want Katie. Now.

KATIE! KATIE!

Now Grace is getting all agitated. She does that when I shout and she can't understand. No, Grace. No! Not a drink, not a story, not a different programme on the TV. KATIE! I want Katie!

Something's happening in the house. Something that shouldn't be happening at all.

I can feel at the back of my head. That's where I feel things. I can't find the words to describe my back-of-the-head feelings but when I get them, I know they mean something. I got one before Dad died; I knew that afternoon that Dad wouldn't come in for his tea, wouldn't pick me up and sing 'Tom, Tom the Piper's Son'. It was like a big jolt that started in the back of my head and then sped all through my body and out at the tips of my toes.

I cried and shouted and banged my fists on the wall but no one took any notice. Mum just gave me a drink in the cup with a lid and said I was having a bad day. Katie put some music on the stereo to cheer me up. You don't get cheered up when the back-of-the-head feelings come. They mean something. They come with messages. You can't just send them away with a drink of blackcurrant and marching music.

KATIE! WHERE ARE YOU? If I scream really loudly, she will come. If I kick as well, and rock backwards in my chair, maybe Grace will call Katie and say she needs help with me. Perhaps if I did something really bad, something I haven't done for a long time, Katie would come even quicker.

KATIE!

Plant pot. Full of mud. On the floor. Yuk.

KATIE!

Now Grace's saying it doesn't matter and she'll get a cloth. I want it to matter, can't she see that? I want Katie. Now.

They think I'm stupid, you know. Even Katie, and Katie's nicer to me than anyone. Nicer even than Mum. Mum's the safest, Katie's the nicest. Mum shouts but not at me. I don't like it when she shouts at Katie but it's quite a safe thing to happen because it has a pattern to it. I like patterns. You know where you stand with patterns. The pattern when Mum shouts is always the same. She shouts at Katie, then Katie yells back, then Mum throws something or hits Katie, then Katie runs off, and I cry and rock about. So Mum wraps her arms round me and we rock together. Ten rocks sometimes, other times more. I can't count more in my head, so I just count them in tens.

That's when Mum starts talking. Softly, softly, so softly that you have to almost stop breathing to hear her.

'Poor little man, poor trapped little man,' she says. That's me – the little man. I know that because she strokes my cheek and kisses the top of my head. 'Just like me, trapped, trapped, trapped!'

I don't know what it means – trapped – but it must be a good thing to be because Mum's like it too, and she can do practically anything. She can cook fried chicken and chips and make boats out of paper and talk on the telephone so that people understand what she's saying. And when she has a screaming crying day, she can make the screams and the sobbing stop when the doorbell rings or the window cleaner comes. Just like that. At once.

I can't do that.

Once the shouting starts, it just carries on till it decides to stop. I don't mind – when the shouting comes I don't feel invisible any more. I open my mouth and the anger and scary feelings and the red hot burning pain pour out onto the floor and flow all over the carpet and then I feel all empty and cold and still.

That's when I just sit and watch. I watch different things. I like watching the wallpaper. It's yellow and white and if you stare for a long time the white bits move and make shapes and patterns.

Like I said, I like patterns.

Now Grace has got the cloth and is wiping up the mud. She still hasn't called Katie so there's nothing for it. I must get hurt.

Hurting brings people fast. It never fails.

'Katie, love! Come down here quick, can you?' Grace sounds scared already and I have only done three bangs. Head banging always works. Sometimes you can make the back-of-the-head feelings go away if you bang hard enough because the pain drives the other feeling away. So it's quite a useful thing really.

I can hear Katie coming. Clip, clop, clomp, jump. She always jumps down the last three stairs. I can't jump. Katie can.

Now I can smell her coming into the room. It's a sort of dry, woody smell and it's not her usual one. Usually she smells of the seaside and windy days; but this smell is different. Everything's different. The new smell of Katie is bringing the back-of-the-head feeling back again.

KATIE! KATIE!

She puts her hands on my shoulders.

'Tom, stop it! What is it, Tom? Tell Katie.'

I stop.

Look at her.

She's gazing at me, her forehead puckered in a frown, her pointy chin jutting out as she leans towards me.

'Tom?'

And then I know.

It's her. The something different that's happening is happening to Katie.

It's going on inside her head and her face looks different because she's thinking about the something and not really thinking about me.

26

WHAT'S HAPPENING, KATIE?

'It's OK, Tom, hush, it's OK,' she says.

But it's not OK.

I have to do something to stop the thing happening, but I don't know how. If Dad was here, Dad would know what to do. Dad knew everything. Dad could even make Mum stop crying.

Sometimes.

DAD! DAD! WANT YOU, DAD!

Katie's gripping my arm. She sits down on the floor beside me, and sticks her legs out in front of her for me to sit on. She's got her shiny new trainers on; silver like the balls on the tree in the window at Christmas time.

'Dad's not here, Tom,' she says, pulling me onto her lap.

'Is that what he's asking for then?' mutters Grace.

Katie nods. Katie knows what my sounds mean. Or at least, some of them.

'Dad's not here, Tom,' she says again.

I know he's not. But if I screw up my eyes tightly and hold my breath I can almost believe he is. I can smell him. I can feel the roughness of his old gardening jacket against my fingers. Hear him sucking on those extra strong mints he likes. Used to like.

'Bless him,' says Grace. 'Missing his dad.'

She takes my hand and looks straight into my eyes. Not many people do that.

'Never mind, Tom love,' she says. 'You've got your mum. And Katie.'

And I see it. Out of the corner of my eye, a long thin black shadow, darting in a flash across Katie's face.

'You love your Katie, don't you?' coos Grace.

I turn and look at Katie.

For just a minute our eyes meet. The shadow darts again. Then she looks away.

27

So now I know for sure.

Something really is happening to Katie – and what's more, she knows what it is.

And she wants it to happen.

It's not a happy-making thing. It's a bad thing. Dark. Spiky.

But it's going to happen and there is nothing at all that I can do about it.

DAD! DAD! DAD!

But Dad has gone.

Like they said, he's dead. Dead means you get taken away and people cry and no one ever sees you again.

I don't know where you go. No one told me that. They just gave me a spoonful of sticky medicine and told me to stay with Grace, and then they drove off in black cars and came back and had egg sandwiches and cups of tea.

No one said where Dead was or how you got there.

But you don't come back from Dead. They told me that.

'Listen, Tom, Mum's back!'

Katie tips me off her lap and jumps up, shaking me, smiling and pointing towards the hall.

I can hear the front door bang, hear Mum sighing as she kicks her shoes off, hear them fall, one, two, onto the floor of the hall cupboard.

I can still smell my dad. But he's not here.

They've told me that dead means gone away forever. So I know that no matter what it feels like, he's not here really.

Like I said, I'm not stupid.

GRACE
Thursday June 28th
8.40 p.m.

Thank heavens she's back. I think I'm getting too old for this child minding lark.

I do hope that Lydia doesn't get too upset about the stain on the carpet. He can't help it, bless him, but he is a handful.

'There, there, Tom, your mum's back!' I go to pat him on the shoulder and then remember that you mustn't touch him – not when he's in one of his moods.

I have to admit that I'm beginning to wonder whether Bill wasn't right. 'Don't you go getting involved' – that's what he said when Lydia announced she was moving to the village. We've been friends ever since we were kids. The age gap never mattered in those days; I was fourteen when she came to the children's home and she was just five, but when you're lonely and feeling like you are rubbish, you latch on to anyone, and for some reason, Lyddy idolised me from the start and that made me feel needed and worth something. Mrs Brophy, our housemother, got me to walk her to the primary school each morning on my way to the girls' school and I soon found out that she was quite grown up for her age. Of course, back then I didn't realise that the poor kid had little chance to be anything else what with her background; I just decided to take her under my wing and look after her. It made me feel important and I liked that.

Anyway, Bill was adamant that you can't let people take over your life and when Lydia left Kettleborough to come to Hartfield, I soon realised that it's easier when someone lives five miles away and can't be hammering on your back door at all hours. Bill doesn't like that; mind you, he's always been a loner; never one for joining clubs or having people round. He would much rather be up in the attic with his train set than having a natter with friends. Well, to be honest, he doesn't have many friends, not these days. It wasn't always like that, mind – when he worked at Claytons, he used to enjoy a pint down the pub with his mates – he even played in the darts team when they were short. But after he got made redundant, he sort of went into himself and now – well, he's not been himself for a long while, not really.

Still, I'm not complaining. He's a good man – and he's company, someone to cuddle up with in the night. That's what Lydia needs, if you ask me; poor soul, losing her husband when she has two kiddies to bring up and one of them not quite right in the head. Oh, I know – you're not supposed to say that these days, are you? Learning difficulties, that's the phrase now. But it's more than that with little Tom – to tell the truth, I think that deep down, he's a bright boy. Don't ask me why I say that because I don't know. It's just a feeling. The way he looks at you sometimes, it's as though he knows it all, but just can't find the words. Not that he looks at you very often; Lydia says it's something to do with his condition – he doesn't connect with people. I love him, just the same.

Of course, if I'm totally honest, Tom was one of the reasons that Bill didn't want me to get too involved with Lydia. Bill's not comfortable with handicap; it's not that he doesn't feel sorry for the disabled – he's the first one to put his hand in his pocket when they come collecting for Mencap or the Blind. It's just that he doesn't know how to talk to people who aren't like him. I guess that's why we never see Gareth any more, but that's another story.

I suppose the reason why I love coming over here and keeping an eye on the kids is because they fill the gap that

Gareth left behind. I always wanted lots of children but it wasn't to be. I can't help thinking that if I'd been born half a century later, I could have had all this fertility treatment and I wouldn't be so lonely now. But God knows what he's doing, I guess. Most of the time.

Here she comes – my, she looks tired! I'll just get the brandy out – she likes a little tot in the evenings and to tell the truth, I could do with one myself.

Tom's lovely, but he can be scary at times.

Not that I'd admit that to anyone else, of course. I like to feel needed.

KATIE
Thursday June 28th
10.30 p.m.

Terrific. Thanks to Tom and his outburst, all my plans have been scuppered and Mum's on red alert. I shouldn't be cross with Tom, I know that. It wasn't his fault. He can't help getting those screaming attacks; Mrs Ostler, his teacher at Lime Lodge, says that it's all down to his frustration at not being able to get through to us, make us see what it is he wants. She says we have to be patient. But then, she doesn't live with him. And he hasn't just messed up all her plans.

Sometimes I wish he hadn't been born.

No. No, I didn't mean that. I can almost see Dad rubbing his chin, the way he used to if he was upset, and saying 'Oh, Princess, you don't mean that really!' I don't, not really. It's just that Dad's gone, and I'm here, and Tom's difficult and Mum's – well, Mum.

And sometimes I feel so alone. Like now.

Things started going wrong around nine o'clock. Mum arrived home at just the wrong moment. There was Tom, thrashing about and shouting, me trying to calm him down and Grace sweeping up the remains of the earth from the pot plant that Tom had hurled onto the floor and muttering to herself, the way she does.

'What the hell is going on?' Mum snapped the moment she stuck her head round the sitting-room door. 'Why isn't Tom in bed?'

I could see she was in a bad mood, the way her mouth was pinched in a thin line and her fingers were pulling at the neck of her jacket.

'Hi, Mum!' I began as brightly as I could. 'It's OK, Tom was just...'

'Oh sure!' she retorted, flinging her handbag onto the sofa. 'It looks bloody OK!'

With that, Tom began rocking backwards and forwards in his chair, moaning and drumming his fingers on the arm.

'Tom!' Mum dropped to her knees in front of him and tried to catch his eye. 'Tom, stop it! Now!'

Tom stared at the wallpaper and grunted.

She turned to Grace.

'Has Katie been upsetting Tom?' she demanded, as if I made a habit of irritating my brother.

'No of course she hasn't, Lyddy,' replied Grace in that soothing voice she uses whenever Mum has a go at me. 'He just got himself a bit upset, that's all. Missing his dad, that's what Katie reckons it is.'

'Oh, does she?' spat my mother, throwing a sideways glance in my direction. 'Little Miss Expert now, is she? And how does she work that one out?'

You could see that poor Grace was dead embarrassed but she did try to stick up for me.

'Katie understands what he says much better than I do,' she volunteered. 'Really good with him, she is. Bless her!'

My mother sniffed and marched over to the sideboard.

'Well, she has to be good at something, I suppose, considering how she's making a complete mess of her education.'

She grabbed the brandy bottle that Grace had put out.

'Never have I been so humiliated as I was this evening,' she said, pouring a generous slug into a goblet. 'All those teachers telling me how you never work, and how hopeless you are.'

'That's not fair!' I began. It's not – I do work. It's just that recently nothing seems to stay inside my head. It is as if it's so full of thoughts and fears and worries that there's no room for rift valleys and the Vietnam War and integers and stuff.

'It's you that's not being fair, young lady!' shouted my mother. 'After all I've been through, I would have thought the least you could do was pull your weight at school. Brandy, Grace?'

'Well, I...'

'Of course you will,' my mother answered for her, pouring another, rather less generous tot into a glass and turning back to me.

'After all your father did for you,' she went on. 'Slaving day and night to give you a decent education, wearing himself to a frazzle. Dear, dear man...'

She bowed her head and her shoulders shook slightly.

Grace rushed over to her. I stood where I was. I'd seen it all before.

'There, there, dear,' soothed Grace putting an arm round Mum's shoulders. 'Don't distress yourself.'

Mum tilted her chin in a sort of 'I must be brave' kind of way and dabbed at her eyes. There wasn't a tear in sight but to someone like Grace, who sees the good in everyone, it must have looked pretty convincing.

'And me,' Mum went on, 'the things I went without so that Katie could have everything she needed.'

Another little sob escaped her lips.

'Put the kettle on, Katie!' ordered Grace sternly, as if suddenly realising that I was the Devil in disguise. 'Your mum's upset.'

So what's new? I wanted to shout at her, but of course I didn't. I went to the kitchen, filled the kettle and plugged it in. I knew it was a waste of time; once Mum got the taste of alcohol on her lips, the last thing she would fancy would be a cup of PG Tips.

'Shall I put Tom to bed?' I offered as I walked back into the sitting room. 'While you and Grace relax and have a drink.'

I make myself sick sometimes, I sound so nauseatingly good; but I had my reasons.

'That's a kind thought,' said Grace. 'Katie's a good girl really.'

My mother sniffed as if to imply that anyone who believed in my righteousness was in need of immediate psychiatric help, but she shrugged her shoulders and nodded.

'Do that,' she said. 'And then I want a word with you.'

That didn't worry me too much. If I took my time sorting Tom out, she and Grace would be onto their third drink and Mum would be in her sentimental, motherly mood. That's when she's at her most manageable. Wait till the fifth drink and you don't stand a chance.

Funnily enough, it was Mum's need for a drink that brought Joe and me together again. I got to thinking about that while I was helping Tom get ready for bed. He has to do everything in this strict routine, otherwise he gets confused. Clothes off, then his cars lined up on the bed. Teeth cleaned, top ones first, then a drink, then bottom ones. It's dead boring standing there, checking on him, but it gives you plenty of time to think.

For the whole week after Joe dropped me off at school I just could not get him out of my mind. That was odd for me, because to be honest, I've never been obsessed with boys. Not like Alice, whose entire life is geared to whichever guy she happens to be in love with at the time. I've been out with a couple, but it's never amounted to much except the odd kiss and a bit of rather boring fumbling.

But with Joe it was different. He hadn't even touched me, and yet when I went to bed each night, I would curl up in a ball and imagine what it would be like to be close to him, to have him run his fingers down the back of my neck or brush his lips across mine. That was the good part; the worst part was that as each day went by, I found it harder and harder to picture what he looked like. Apart from his eyes, of course; I wasn't likely to forget those. But I could no longer hear the sound of his voice in my head or remember how he looked when he laughed. Yet, despite all that, I couldn't get him out of my mind.

I started leaving home earlier and earlier each morning so that I could walk up the Frampton Road and catch the bus two stops before my usual one. I figured that he must take the same route when he came to see his mate, and with a bit of luck I might accidentally on purpose bump into him. Alice, of course, wanted to know why I was suddenly catching the bus at Spectacle Lane instead of outside the post office but I just told her that I'd found some cellulite on my thighs and needed more exercise.

Days went by and I didn't see Joe. Then the following Saturday, Mum had a real mega bad mood crash. I could see it coming and I did everything I could to stop it. I took Tom out to the park, which is something I hate doing because if he gets one of his shouting attacks, people look at me as if I'm murdering him or something. I know it's wicked of me, but sometimes I wish that Tom looked different from other ten-year-old boys, but he doesn't. He has these huge blue eyes and long lashes and a mop of wavy blond hair and anyone who didn't know would think he was perfectly normal. And he will sit on a bench in the park for ages, sketching things. Not just ordinary things either; he'll see a tiny little insect on the path and painstakingly draw it, adding details long after the ant or the earwig or whatever it is has scuttled away. And the drawings are good, which is another problem. Sometimes passers-by will stop and look over his shoulder, and because he looks like any other little boy, they will start talking to him.

'My!' they will say. 'That's a lovely picture.'

And then sometimes they will point to it and touch the paper and that does it. Tom goes manic. He jumps up, snatches the drawing, shouts, shakes his head and creates a real fuss. Then of course, I have to explain about how he is autistic and has all sorts of problems, and the people nod and disappear and I'm left to calm him down and get him home.

I don't know why he acts like that. I mean, it's not as if the people tell him that his drawings are rubbish. Most kids like to be praised and made a fuss of, regardless of who is doing it. But Tom's only ever been happy with me or Mum or Grace. And Dad of course. But Dad's not here any more.

I was wishing Dad was around that Saturday when Mum had her mood crash. When I got Tom home from the park, she was rummaging around in the drinks cupboard, cursing and swearing because there were only about three centimetres of brandy left in the bottom of the bottle. Her hands were shaking and she was crying in great jerky gulps.

I just wanted Dad to appear at the door and take over. He never liked the way Mum drank, and sometimes – not always – he could divert her attention a bit, just by giving her a white wine and soda in a long glass and then taking her shopping or telling her that he needed her help with something. I've tried that but it never works.

In the end, I was glad that she needed more brandy because if she hadn't sent me up to the shop, I wouldn't have been in the Co-op. And if the girl at the checkout hadn't made such a fuss, Joe would never have spotted me.

It was weird. He wasn't in the shop as I dashed up and down the aisles, searching for the brandy. I know he wasn't: he's not the kind of guy you miss. Anyway, I found the brandy and threw the ten-pound note at the girl on the checkout.

'Age?' she yawned.

'What?'

'Have you got ID?' she said. 'I can't sell you this if you're under age.'

I tapped my foot impatiently.

'It's not for me, it's for my mother. She's ill,' I said, bending the truth slightly.

She shrugged.

'Still can't sell it,' she said. 'You'll have to get someone else to buy it for her. Sorry.'

I knew just how Mum would react if I got home without her precious alcohol. When she gets the shakes, she just sits and cries till she has had enough brandy to steady her. And when she can't get it, she goes really mad.

And it's nearly always at me.

'There isn't anyone else!' I shouted. 'My dad is dead, my brother's – well, he's too little, so it's down to me. Get it?'

The girl shrugged.

'The law's the law,' she said. 'Sorry.'

I was almost in tears. I snatched up the note, and that's when I felt a hand on my shoulder.

'It's OK,' said a deep voice. 'I'll buy the brandy for Mrs Fordyce.'

I spun round and there he was. Joe. He was wearing an open-necked shirt with just the tiniest bit of fluffy hair peeking through. He looked divine.

He smiled at me and winked. I was speechless. I could feel the colour flooding my cheeks and I wished I'd put make-up on before I left the house.

The checkout girl looked doubtful.

'Mrs Fordyce is a good friend of mine,' Joe said. 'I'll make sure that this goes straight into her hands and no one else's.'

He beamed at the girl and she turned bright pink, flicked a piece of hair out of her eyes and pouted her lips.

'OK, then,' she said breathily, gazing up at him from under her eyelashes.

He took a twenty-pound note from his pocket.

'I've got the money,' I began but he waved my hand away.

The girl rang the till and gave him his change. Resting his hand lightly on my shoulder, and picking up the brandy with his other hand, he ushered me out of the shop.

'Thanks ever so much,' I began. 'But you must let me pay.'

He shook his head.

'You keep the money,' he said. 'I'd like to pay for it. I know what it's like.'

I remember how my stomach lurched at his words.

'What do you mean?' I asked.

He sighed.

'You're a very brave person,' he said solemnly. 'But I recognise pain when I see it, and I guess you've had more than your fair share.'

He looked at me so gently and sounded so understanding that I felt my eyes filling with tears. I looked away quickly.

'She was always a bitch – my mum, that is,' he said softly. 'With yours it's the drink' – he waved the brandy bottle – 'with mine it was – oh, well, never mind.'

I swallowed. I didn't really know what to say, but it was OK, because he suddenly broke into a broad grin.

'But that's all in the past now,' he said cheerfully. 'Come on, we'd better get this brandy back to your mum because ...'

'Oh, it's fine!' I said hurriedly. 'I'll take it.'

I stretched out my hand but Joe shook his head.

'I promised to deliver it,' he said, pulling a pair of really flash shades from his shirt pocket. 'You don't want to get the girl in the shop into trouble, do you? She can't be much older than you.'

I bit my lip. To be honest, I didn't want Joe to meet my mum, not while she was in one of her black moods. You never know what she's going to come out with when she's like that.

'Trust me,' he said, slipping the shades over his nose and smiling down at me. 'I'll just come to the door, hand over the bottle and go. OK?'

'OK,' I said, largely because it would mean walking with him for a few hundred yards.

When we got to the house, I fished for my key and unlocked the front door. As it swung open, my heart sank. There was Mum, leaning against the kitchen doorpost, with Tom sitting colouring on the floor beside her.

'About bloody time...oh!'

She caught sight of Joe and stopped. She gasped out loud and her eyes widened.

'Who are you?' she asked abruptly.

'Mrs Fordyce,' exclaimed Joe stepping into the hall. 'How delighted I am to meet you! And this, I think, is for you!'

He handed her the bottle of brandy. Tom stopped drawing and began to rock backwards and forwards, his eyes riveted on Joe.

I held my breath.

'Well yes, I...'

Mum was clearly lost for words and Tom was beginning to rock faster and faster but Joe just kept talking.

'They wouldn't let your daughter buy it,' he said. 'Too young. So I stepped in. And here we are!'

My mother coughed and tightened her grip on the bottle.

'Thank you,' she said. 'That's kind. Very kind.'

She had her eyes fixed on Joe's face, her face puckering in a frown. I was just thankful that she was being polite.

'Well, you enjoy it!' said Joe, looking down at Tom. 'And what's this, little fellow?'

He took the sheet of paper which Tom had dropped onto the floor and gazed at it.

'That's brilliant!' he breathed. 'Absolutely incredible.'

I waited for Tom to scream and snatch the paper. He didn't. He just stared at Joe, and began shuffling backwards on his bottom, through the open kitchen door and back, back until he bumped into the table.

And then he screamed.

Oh boy, did he scream!

'He wants his drawing back,' I said hastily, snatching it from Joe. 'He's a bit – well, he's disturbed and I think he's scared of your sunglasses...'

'Of course,' said Joe easily, turning back to Mum. 'Disturbed. But Mrs Fordyce, you must be so proud of his artistic talent. Does he get it from you?'

My mother actually stood there and preened. She patted her hair and simpered like some bimbo in a third-rate movie.

'Well, I have to say I do have an eye for colour,' she murmured. 'And of course, if life had been different, they do say I could have made something of my creative talents.'

It was the first I had heard of it, but I knew better than to comment.

Joe didn't say anything for a moment, just stood and looked from Mum to Tom's drawing and back again.

'Well, they say talents run in families, don't they?' he remarked eventually. 'Anyway, I must be off – things to do, people to see!'

He turned and I followed him to the front door. I could see that Mum, having done her little bit of showing off, was already ripping at the foil cap of the brandy bottle.

''Bye, Joe,' I whispered. 'Thanks ever so much.'

He leaned towards me.

'You save that money she gave you,' he hissed in my ear. 'No need to tell her I paid. Start a little nest egg – you never know when you might need one.'

And with that he opened the front gate and began striding off up the hill.

'Joe!'

I don't know why I called after him. As he turned, I hadn't a clue what I was going to say.

'Yes?'

'Thanks again,' I said, feeling foolish.

'You're welcome!' he smiled, stuffing his sunglasses back into his pocket. 'See you soon!'

And with that he was gone. I didn't really believe him when he said that he would see me soon. I thought it was just one of those polite things that people say when they can't wait to get away.

But he did see me again, loads of times. I never knew when he was coming, but that's because he never knew when he could get away. He was doing a lot of odd jobs, he told me, trying to find out what he really wanted to do with his life. I didn't care; I was just thankful that he hadn't got tired of me.

I didn't tell anyone. Mum, of course, had wanted to know all about him the moment he left that day – where I'd met him, who he was, the works. I lied. I said he was the brother of Antonia, one of my school mates. She approves of Ant, but it didn't stop her going on about me being too young to hang around with guys; I just nodded and said I wasn't interested, and by then she'd had a couple of brandies and lost interest.

As I stood there tonight, watching Tom going through his ritual of lining up his cars at the foot of his bed, and then turning them all upside down, one by one, I thought about how secretive I had been over Joe. Mum never mentioned him after that day probably because after drinking half the bottle of brandy, she had forgotten that he existed. I admit I used to tell Tom things about him, about our secret meetings and how much I loved him – but of course Tom won't remember and even if he does, it won't mean anything to him.

I did begin to tell Alice once, after Joe and I got really close, but she started asking loads of questions and wanting

42

to meet him, and suddenly I realised that Joe was the only thing in my life that was totally and completely mine. I didn't want to share him – I didn't even want to share anything about him.

So I shut up.

Whenever Alice asked questions, I would just shrug and make out I didn't want to talk about it, so that she'd think he'd dumped me. She never mentions it now and that's the way I want it to be.

Only it would be nice if just one person knew what was going on, because now that all my plans are turned upside down, I need an ally and I haven't got anyone. Just Joe. And until tomorrow morning, I can't get in touch with Joe. I can't risk Mum hearing me talking on the phone. I haven't even got a mobile phone any more; Mum did get me one but I lost it and now she says I'm too immature to be trusted.

I was so sure, as I went back downstairs after saying good-night to Tom, that I could twist Mum round my little finger. I could hear her and Grace droning on and on in that slightly slurred way that people talk when they are onto their third drink. I even heard Mum laugh a couple of times and Grace telling her that she was a great sort. Mum thrives on compliments so I guessed that my moment had come.

I pushed open the sitting-room door, put my best smile on my face and sat down on the beanbag opposite Mum.

'Mum,' I said sweetly, 'Mandy Russell is having a sleepover tomorrow night and she's asked me to go. Her dad will bring me back on Saturday morning; that's OK, isn't it?'

'Nope!' she said, with a silly grin on her face and took another slurp of brandy. 'You are not going anywhere. Nowhere. Not at all.'

I could see she was just at the edge of the being nice bit and heading towards the getting bolshy bit.

'Little girls who do bad homework don't go to parties,' she

said in a sing-song voice, and topped up her glass. 'That's true, isn't it, Grace?'

Poor Grace looked at Mum and then at me, and then at the clock.

'Gracious!' she cried in mock surprise. 'Is that the time? I must be going – there's the dog to walk and the cat to feed.'

With that, she jumped up and started gathering up her bag and her knitting.

'Mum, please!' I said hastily, willing Grace to stay put for just another minute or two. 'You see, Mandy's got this new software package for her computer – GCSE revision course, it is – and we're all going to have a go with it and see if we can get our History project work sussed.'

I've never talked such a load of rubbish in my entire life, but at least it had an effect on Grace.

'Ah!' she said. 'There you are, Lyddy. I told you Katie wasn't one to drop out. You're going to work hard for your mum, aren't you, Katie, dear?'

No! I wanted to shriek. I'm not going to do anything for her. If I work, it will be for me. Just for me.

But instead, I smiled meekly and nodded.

'I'm sorry about the grades, Mum,' I said. 'I've been missing Dad so much and my concentration has been awful and . . .'

'Oh, so you've been missing your dad, have you?' cried my mother suddenly bursting into tears. 'And what about me? Struggling day and night to raise two children, friendless, alone, barely enough to live on, torn apart with grief . . .'

'There, there, dear,' murmured Grace, tapping Mum's shoulder and looking anxiously at the clock. 'I would stay, dear, but really if I don't get back . . .'

'Go!' Mum waved her hand in the air. 'I'll be fine. Don't worry about me. I'm a survivor. Dr Maddocks says he's never seen such courage in a widow before and the man from the *Echo* – the one at the funeral who took the details for the paper . . .'

She was off. I nodded briefly at Grace and with a look of relief washing over her face, she retreated rapidly from the room without a backward glance.

The moment that Mum heard the front door click closed, she stopped her wailing, stood up and came towards me.

'Do you know how humiliated I felt at that school tonight?' she asked, her eyes narrowing as she looked at me. 'Those teachers were trying to imply that you were falling behind with your work because of me, because I wasn't doing things right.'

By now she was standing right up against me, her eyes just centimetres from mine.

'What,' she asked in a quiet voice, 'have you been saying to them?'

I started to feel sick.

'Nothing, Mum,' I whispered. 'Honestly. Nothing.'

It was the truth. I've never told anyone what Mum is really like. I've never admitted that living at home is hell at times and that I wished I had the courage to run away and never, ever go back.

It's not the sort of thing you say to people. I love Mum. I don't like her, and I hate what she does. But I love her. She's my mum.

And when she's nice, she's really nice. It's just that when she isn't, she terrifying.

'Am I not a good mother to you – yes or no?' she demanded.

'Yes,' I whispered.

'Do I keep you short of food?'

'No, Mum.'

'Do I stop you going out and buying yourself nice clothes?'

I shook my head.

'Who was it said yes to those crazy silver trainers you went on and on about?' She grabbed my shoulders. 'Who was it?'

'You, Mum,' I whispered. I couldn't help feeling guilty;

those trainers cost a bomb and I never expected her to let me have them.

'So,' she spat, and I knew the crunch was coming. 'Is it too much to ask you to make an effort to do well at school, to be a credit to me? Heaven knows, poor Tom isn't going to amount to much, and your dad is dead. I'm depending on you.'

I know it's babyish to cry when you are fifteen years old, but I couldn't help it. It was those words 'your dad is dead' that did it. How could she stand there and go on about him dying and her depending on me, after what she had said and done at the weekend? All those confused feelings that had swamped me four days before welled up in me again and I couldn't stop crying.

'Please, Mum, let me go to Mandy's!' I sobbed.

Of course, I didn't want to go to Mandy's. Mandy was just going to prove a very convenient alibi, not that she realises it. But I had to get Mum to think that's where I would be spending Friday night because it was all part of Joe's plan.

Joe's plan for my escape.

'No, you are bloody not going anywhere!' screamed my mother, lunging her face towards mine so that my eyes watered with the brandy fumes. 'You are bloody staying here and looking after me, for once! And working! Working! Working! Get it!'

She sank down in the armchair and I knew it wouldn't be long before she fell asleep. There was no point in saying anything else.

As her eyelids began to droop, I flung a cotton throw over her knees and went upstairs to my room. As I passed Tom's door, I could hear him humming monotonously on one note. Normally I would have opened the door and said goodnight, but I couldn't be bothered. He hates to see me upset and frankly, I couldn't muster the energy to look cheerful.

That was an hour ago. He's quiet now. Everything's quiet.

I guess Mum is asleep in the armchair and she will wake up in the morning in a foul mood because her back hurts and her clothes are creased and she's got a blinding headache.

Tough.

I sound well hard, but I'm not. I'm scared. I can't stick to our original plan, because if she sees me walking off to school with that big blue holdall in my hand, she will think that I'm planning to stay the night at Mandy's and she'll stop me. But I can't leave the holdall behind, because Joe says we'll be away for at least a week and I need the clothes and the cash and stuff.

I've got to go and I've got to think of a way to take the stuff with me.

I suppose I could go now. While she's asleep. The drink won't wear off yet – she'll be dead to the world for at least another couple of hours.

At half past eight tomorrow, I'll be on a bus to Milton Keynes and there I'll meet Joe and we'll set off for Foxhole Farm.

And for a whole week I won't have to be scared.

If I go now, I'll have to find somewhere to spend the night but at least I'll be away.

No! No! That's a dumb idea.

If I'm not here for breakfast, Mum will guess that I've done a runner and raise the alarm. Joe says we must make sure we have as much time as possible before she realises that anything is wrong. Act as normal as possible, he said.

Hang on. That's it. I've got it!

Why didn't I think of it before?

It's brilliant. It can't fail. And as long as Mum stays asleep for just a little bit longer, I'll be home and dry.

Sussed.

TOM
Thursday June 28th
11.10 p.m.

It's black. All black, except for the little round light in the corner of the room. Night light, that's what it's called. I know that because Katie told me. Night light, night light. A good sound. A sound with a pattern. I like patterns.

I like the pattern on my bedroom curtains, the shadows waving gently in the light of the street lamp. Sometimes they move fast, and sometimes they don't move at all. Katie says it's the wind that makes the shadows move and there's nothing to be frightened of. Once, when they thought I was scared, Katie said I could have her bedroom, because it's at the back of the house and there are no flickering lights. They even started moving my stuff but I wasn't having that. I like patterns. I'd hate a room with no patterns.

If I press my hands hard against my eyes, I see dots and sprinkles and swirly shapes, red and orange and gold – patterns coming from inside me. These are the best patterns, the ones I can find when I'm all alone and people don't start speaking to me and taking things and making noises I can't understand.

If I rub my ears with the tips of my fingers, it makes a nice noise, like the seashell noise I heard when we went to the beach with Dad and he put a shell to my ear. A going-to-sleep sound, gentle and quiet and comforting, like putting your thumb in your mouth or...

What's that? A noise. A wrong noise. Not a normal, in-bed-waiting-to-go-to-sleep noise – an outside the house noise. Not a car, not the cat from next door wailing and hissing on

48

the garden fence, not the church clock bonging and chiming. It's a creeping sound, a clicking sound, a rustling sound.

Mustn't get out of bed. Boys don't get out of bed in the night unless they need the bathroom. But I want to see the noise. And if I get out of bed, I might need the bathroom. So that would be all right.

It's cold. Cold feet, shivery knees. Pull back the curtains just a bit.

Someone's out there. Someone moving.

It's Katie.

Katie's out there in the dark. That's not right. Katie doesn't belong out there in the dark in her red pyjamas. Katie belongs in the house at night. That's the pattern. That's the way it is.

'KATIE!'

Bang the window, make her hear.

She's wearing her silver trainers. You don't wear trainers with pyjamas; you wear slippers. And she's carrying one of those rubbish bags, the kind Mum puts in the dustbin, all black and shiny. The rubbish doesn't go out in the night. The rubbish goes out in the morning when the milk comes in. That's the way it is.

I must tell Katie she's got it all wrong. Bang harder, shout louder.

She's looking up. She looks scared.

Wave your arms, keep banging.

She's opening the front gate, throwing the bag onto the pavement, kicking it out of sight. Now she's looking up at me and putting her finger up to her lips.

I don't understand. I don't, I don't!

KATIE!

There's a door banging. Footsteps on the stairs. Not Mum. Mum's are plodding and heavy. These are fast and pitter pattery. It's Katie. Katie's coming. That's right. She should be upstairs because it's night time.

'Tom!'

She's standing in the doorway, the light from the landing making her hair look shiny. Her cheeks are pink, much pinker than usual and she's panting, as though she is out of breath.

'Tom!' She comes over to me and takes my hand, leads me back to bed. 'What are you doing?'

I try to tell her, the rubbish doesn't go out in the night. It's not the right pattern. You must keep to the pattern. But she doesn't understand, or she doesn't listen. I am not sure which.

'I've been having a clear out,' she says. 'Throwing away stuff I don't need any more.'

I shake my head. I'm not sure what she's saying but she has to understand. She's doing it all wrong.

She looks at me and ruffles my hair.

'Hey, calm down!' she whispers. 'It's OK – everything's all right.'

It's not.

I know it's not.

The bad head feeling is coming on and I try to rock it away. Faster, faster. Rock, rock.

'Oh Tom, don't!' She puts her arms round me and hugs me. 'You will be all right, won't you?'

I push her away. It's not all right. It's all wrong. The pattern of the night has gone wrong and that's bad.

She cups my face in her hands and stares at me.

'I have to do this, Tom,' she whispers. 'I have to go . . .'

Go? Not go! No. Katie must stay here. That's where Katie belongs. Here. If I shout she'll understand. She has to understand.

'Hush, Tom, you'll wake Mum!' Katie shakes me, her face all screwed-up in one big frown. 'It'll be OK – I'll come back. I'm going on a little holiday. Just for a week or so, to the farm with Joe, and then I'll be home. OK?'

I rock faster but she doesn't seem to notice. She's staring out of the window.

'Foxhole Farm,' she whispers. 'Foxhole. Doesn't that sound lovely, Tom? There might be animals, like on your toy farm, remember?'

Horses. Pigs. Dogs.

'And Joe says that he and me are going for long walks in the woods and we're going to . . . Tom, stop it!'

Not Joe. The Joe man is not nice, not kind. His mouth smiles but in his head, he's bad.

'Tom, be quiet!'

But I won't stop it. Shout, shout, kick, bang.

Katie puts her hand over my mouth. Horrid, don't like it.

'OK, Tom, I won't go away. I'll stay here. Katie will stay. Shush, now.'

She touches my fingertips.

'I'll stay, Tom. Go to sleep, now. There's a good boy.'

I look up at her.

'It's OK,' she says. But she knows it's not. And I know too. Like I say, I'm not stupid.

LYDIA
Friday June 29th
7.15 a.m.

I'm going to die. I know I am. I've never felt this ill in my whole life. My head feels as if it is about to explode and I know that if I move an inch, I'll throw up.

It must have been that pork pie I had for supper. It sat heavy the moment I'd eaten it. I bet that was the cause of the nightmare too. It must have been – I haven't dreamed about – well, any of those things for months. I dreamed about my dad and the little baby and then about Him and how he used to hit me. It was awful.

Katie says I screamed out loud. 'No, no, I didn't mean to – please, leave me alone!' That's what she told me I was yelling.

'Mum, you're dreaming!' Her words sounded as if they were coming from far away. ' It's OK – it's just a bad dream!' She must have been shaking me, trying to wake me up but of course, I was still dreaming and thought it was Him and that made me shriek all the louder.

And then, when I did come to my senses, the room was going round and I felt sick to my stomach and all tearful and shaky. It didn't help that Tom was standing in the doorway, pulling at his pyjama buttons and whimpering the way he does when there's any sort of commotion. I knew I should get up and go to him, but I felt so dreadful I couldn't move. That's when Katie said she'd bring me some tea.

She'll be back in a minute and then I'll get her to deal with Tom. He's sitting on the end of my bed, rocking back and forth and making that awful wailing noise, the one he makes when he's frightened. I've told him I'm fine, but it doesn't seem to make any difference. Some days, you think you're getting through to him, and then on others, it's like talking to a brick wall.

Here comes Katie now. Good heavens, she's brought a tray with a cloth on, and toast and everything. Of course, she's trying to get on the right side of me, make me forget how badly she's doing at school. Still, it's nice. Perhaps she's finally mending her ways. Not that I could eat a morsel; my stomach's going over and over like nobody's business.

'You've got to eat, Mum,' she says in that dictatorial way she has at times. 'It'll settle your stomach.'

'I can't eat, I've got food poisoning,' I tell her through gritted teeth. I'm afraid if I speak properly, I'll vomit right here on the duvet.

'Brandy poisoning more like!' she retorts, tossing her head and sticking out her chin. 'You stink of the stuff!'

That's nonsense, of course. I mean, I didn't have that much – just enough to relax me and help me sleep. Patronising little madam – so much for thinking she was mending her ways. I'd give her a mouthful if I had the energy.

'Why do you do it, Mum?' She's plonked herself down on the bed and taken my hand. 'Why? You know it makes you feel dreadful the next day.'

What can I say? How can I explain? She wouldn't understand – couldn't understand. She's only a kid, after all; what does she know of the pain and the hurt and the misery of it all? Brandy takes the ache away – just for a couple of hours, I can feel like a normal forty-six-year-old, have a laugh, sing a song. I can forget about Tom not being like other lads, and about Jarvis messing up and dying. And I can forget about Him. It's not much, but it's all I've got.

But I can't expect Katie to understand all that.

'Mum?' She leans forward and watches me anxiously, thrusting the plate of toast in my direction.

'Deal with Tom, love,' I whisper, almost gagging on the words as the smell of Marmite hits my nostrils.

She shakes her head.

'I can't, Mum,' she stresses. 'Haven't time.'

'What do you mean, you ... oh God!' My stomach is heaving itself up into my mouth. I clamp my hand to my mouth, throw back the covers and stagger out onto the landing.

'You're disgusting, Mum!' Katie's voice cracks into a sob that is drowned out by the sound of my own retching.

She's right, though. I am.

Oh God, I am. Disgusting.

A sordid cow.

In between the retching, I can hear her in the other room, murmuring to Tom.

'It's OK, Tom, she'll be OK, don't you worry, Tommy, it's just fine.' She's talking in the sing-song way he likes and I know she's calming him down. 'Mum's OK, Tom, she's just fine.'

Oh sure, I am. But I've got to get myself together. I've got to be on form for Tom.

Tom needs me.

I feel a bit better now. Empty, but better.

'Mum!' Katie's standing in the doorway, her nose wrinkling in disgust as I flush the loo and I realise for the first time that she's already dressed and ready for school. 'Are you all right now? Only I've got to get going ...'

'You can't go yet!' Little madam, thinking she can rush off and leave me to deal with everything. 'Tom's not dressed and there's his breakfast to get – I can't face going near food. You'll have to do it.'

I heave myself up onto my feet and turn on the tap, splashing cold water all over my face.

'But, Mum,' says Katie touching my arm, 'I'm going to school early. You're right, you see – I do need to work harder and I thought that if I went in early each morning and studied in the library I could catch up.'

She looks at me with those huge, strange eyes – eyes just like his.

'Yes, well . . . ' To tell the truth, she's caught me off guard. 'You could start doing that next week. Today I need you here.'

Katie opens her mouth and says something but I can't hear because of the sudden racket outside – the wretched bleeping of a reversing lorry and enough banging and clattering to waken the dead.

'Oh, my head!' I've cried out before I realise it. The noise makes my aching temples throb and the feeling of nausea swamps me again. 'What in the name of heaven is going on?'

'It's the dustcart!' Katie glances at her watch and looks alarmed. 'It's early! I've got to . . . I'll just – there's another rubbish bag to go out. I'll do it!'

And with that, she's gone, clumping down the stairs in those hideous silver trainers she would insist on buying. I can't understand why all these kids want to wear shoes that make their feet look like dinner plates myself, but she seems to think they're just the thing. Of course, she's not allowed to wear them to school; Pipers Court has standards, unlike some schools I could mention.

I must say, Katie does seem to be trying. I mean, normally, she wouldn't notice if a dozen rubbish bags sat in the kitchen for a month of Sundays.

Now Tom's making a song and dance again. Must be the noise that's upset him.

'It's OK, Tom – just a big lorry, nothing to worry about it.' I say it three times, but he ignores me and just wails and rocks. It's going to be one of those days and frankly, I can't take it. When Katie's done the rubbish, I'll have to ask her to get him dressed.

She can't leave everything to me. Not with me feeling so ill. It's a rotten thing, food poisoning

KATIE
Friday June 29th
8.25 a.m.

I've done it! I've actually done it! Thank goodness the bus isn't full – my knees feel like jelly and I can't stop shaking. It's weird – half of me feels elated and excited and the other feels dead scared. And right now, I guess the dead scared half is winning.

I really thought I'd had it when the dustcart turned up early. I had visions of my holdall disappearing into the van and all my new clothes being crunched to pulp. I only just got there in time; I belted out of the house, and was yanking open the front gate, just as the refuse collection guy began snatching up our bags and hurling them into the back of the cart.

'Not that one!' I called in a loud whisper as his hand hovered over the last bag. I didn't dare shout in case Mum heard.

The guy looked up at me, chewing thoughtfully on some gum.

'What?'

'I don't want that bag to go!' I stressed grabbing it out of his reach.

'Most people,' he said with a lopsided grin, 'don't put rubbish in the street unless they want it to go.'

'It was a mistake,' I mumbled, willing him to get on with his job and let me pass.

He winked at me.

'Love letters, is it? Threw them out in a fit of rage and now you can't bear to part with them? I'll bet that's it!'

'No – yes, something like that!' I tried to look cool and laid back which is pretty difficult when your nostrils are being assailed with the stink of a whole street full of rotting garbage.

'Thought so!' he exclaimed triumphantly.

He resumed his chewing, and to my relief began to edge away.

'I like to make up stories about the things people chuck out,' he called as the van pulled slowly away down the street. 'Makes the job more interesting, like!'

He turned away and continued picking up rubbish bags. I ripped the plastic bag open, grabbed the blue holdall and glanced up at the windows of my house. No one there.

I stuffed the torn bin bag into the hedge next door and set off. I resisted the urge to run all the way to the bus stop; I didn't want to draw attention to myself. Luckily, I didn't have long to wait; the seven forty-five was dead on time and when I got to the bus station, the Milton Keynes Express was already in the bay with the engine running. It's not that full, either, which means I've got a double seat to myself. And in just over an hour I'll be with Joe.

I love him so much. He's so calm and so strong and he always knows just what to do. When he holds me tight, I feel so safe – it's as if nothing in the world can ever get close enough to hurt me again. He says that hurting people is the worst thing anyone can do and that it's time Mum got to feel a bit of the pain she causes other people. When I told him about what happened last weekend, he actually had tears in his eyes. Most guys wouldn't be seen dead crying, but Joe's not like that. He said that my pain was his pain, and my loss was his loss. That was so romantic.

We're out of Kettleborough now and heading for the motorway. This really is it. I'm running away.

It's not like I didn't warn her. I did.

'I can't stand this, Mum!' I yelled last Sunday after she'd hit me and said those awful things. 'One day, I'm going to walk out that door and never, ever come back again!'

Of course, all she did was burst into tears and say that life had sent her too much trouble for one woman to cope with. I didn't say anything more; I couldn't. Her words were still ringing in my ears, making me feel sick to my stomach.

It had started just because she found me in my room crying. I'd gone upstairs because Mum had been in a foul mood all day, and I didn't want to be anywhere near her. I'd been sitting on the floor, looking through photo albums and found some of Dad and me when I was little. There was one of us tobogganing down a steep hill on the Sussex Downs, and another of him teaching me to swim. One minute I was smiling at the pictures and the next, I was crying and that's how she found me.

I knew she'd been drinking the moment she came into the room, just by the way she held onto the door frame and thrust out her chin as if to defy me asking whether she was drunk.

'What's the matter, Pumpkin?' she asked, quite kindly I admit.

'I miss my dad so much,' I sobbed. 'Nothing's the same without him.'

She bristled slightly, and sniffed but didn't say much.

I pushed the photo album across the floor towards her.

'Look!' I said. 'Those are of me and Dad when I was really tiny – before Tom was born.'

She picked up the album and stared at it for a long time.

'Do I look like my dad, do you think?' I asked. I knew the answer really but I still hunt for odd things that I might have inherited from him. I've got Mum's ash blonde hair and her freckles, and sadly I'm stocky like her, not all lithe and athletic like Dad.

'Do you look like your dad?' Mum repeated the words back to me slowly, and I realised she was more tipsy than I had thought. Her speech was slurring and her eyes darted all over the place. 'D'ya look like your dad?'

She looked up at me.

'Why would you want to look like *him*?'

Before I could answer, she had taken two steps towards me.

'I said – why would you want to look like *him*?'

'Because I love him and ...'

She hurled the album to the floor.

'Love? Huh!'

She wiped the back of her hand across her mouth.

'He knew nothing about love, that's for sure!' she spat, grabbing the back of a chair for support. 'Not your dad – oh no! Love you? Oh no – he wouldn't have known how!'

You know how you read in books that people's blood runs cold when they've had a shock? I always thought it was rubbish, but it's true. Mine did. I felt sick and shivery.

'He did so!' I cried. 'He called me his Princess and said that I was the best thing that ever happened to him.'

She stood dead still in the middle of the room, staring at me like I was talking in some foreign language.

'What?'

'Dad!' I spat out the words. 'He did love me – and I miss him and ...'

By now I was crying too much to speak coherently.

'Suit yourself,' she muttered and turned to go out of the room.

'Mum!' I screeched. 'Don't just walk away! Don't you dare tell lies about my dad! My dad was nice to me, which is more than you are! You're the one who doesn't know anything about love, not him! Look at you – a drunken, sozzled mess!'

That's when she hit me. Round the face. Twice.

I guess I deserved it. I shouldn't have said those things about her.

But they were true.

'You little bitch!' she spat. 'Well, I'll tell you one thing; you've certainly turned out like your father. A vicious, nasty...'

She leaned towards me and I could smell the brandy on her breath.

'My dad wasn't nasty!' My words came in short sobs. 'He was lovely, he was gentle and...'

'Him? That overweight, overbearing...'

She swayed slightly and blinked.

'Oh – think what you like! I guess it would have been easier all round if you had never been born!'

And with that she turned and went out of the room.

I don't know how long I stood there. I was shaking with anger. How dare she speak about my dead father like that? Dad was gentle and funny and – OK, a bit of a doormat when it came to dealing with Mum, but I loved him so much.

He wasn't overbearing, and he certainly wasn't fat. Clearly she was even more drunk than I thought she was.

Did she really mean that life would have been better without me? Did my dad think that?

No. I wouldn't believe it. He loved me. I know he did.

By the time I got downstairs, Mum was sitting in a chair, crying.

'I'm sorry, Pumpkin,' she hiccuped. 'I didn't mean to hit you – only you got me all confused.'

Oh sure – like I unscrewed the brandy bottle and poured the stuff down her throat.

I didn't reply. I couldn't.

I told Joe the whole story that evening. We've been meeting regularly for the past few months – every other Tuesday – that's the only time he can get up this way. I told him about what Mum called my dad and how she slapped me and everything. He went very pale and clenched his fists and paced up and down the path in the recreation ground for ages.

'That does it,' he said in the end. 'Now is the time.'

'Time for what?' I asked.

'For you to walk out on her!' He almost spat the words out.

'I can't . . . ' I started.

Joe sighed deeply and put his arm round me.

'Yes you can,' he urged. 'Teach her a lesson.'

I shook my head.

'I can't,' I explained, 'because of Tom. Tom needs me.'

Joe stared at me for a long time and then he smiled.

'Tom's not your problem,' he said softly. 'You can't help other people until your own life is sorted.'

That was when he pulled me towards him, burying my face in his shoulder and kissing the back of my neck.

'Little Katie, poor Katie,' he crooned. 'Trust me. You'll see – it'll change everything, I promise.'

His voice was so gentle and his arms felt so good that I couldn't help crying.

'You believe my dad loved me, don't you?' I whispered through my tears.

He squeezed me tighter – almost too tightly.

'I suppose he must have done, yes!' he said, almost reluctantly.

They weren't quite the words I wanted to hear but I knew he meant them to make me feel better.

We made plans then – these plans that I'm putting into practice right now. Joe said he'd take me to the farm where he lives with a crowd of other people. It's a sort of commune, with students and artists and people like Joe who are chilling out in order to discover what they want to do with their life.

It sounds cool.

He's going to tell them I'm his girlfriend. It sends shivers down my spine just thinking about it. I love him so much.

And in less than an hour, I'll be with him and he'll make everything come right.

He always does.

61

GRACE
Friday June 29th
9.30 a.m.

I've just popped in to see Lydia. I wish I hadn't bothered. Honestly, sometimes there's no pleasing that woman. No sooner am I inside the door than she's going on about Katie leaving early for school without so much as a goodbye.

'Well,' I said as cheerily as I could, 'it shows she means business, doesn't it? I mean, you did want her to apply herself to her studies, didn't you?'

'I wanted her here,' she replied, as truculently as a spoilt five-year-old. 'I'm not too good this morning and I needed her help with Tom and the breakfast and everything.'

She did look pretty groggy, I admit, but frankly, I think it was the drink. She got through four large brandies in the time it took me to sip one tiny one diluted with Coca Cola (and I threw half of that in the rubber plant when she wasn't looking). Bill says I should refuse point blank to drink with her, but as I say to him, it's not as easy as that. She's all alone and sometimes I think that having me to chat to actually stops her losing her rag as often as she might. Mind you, it would be better to do it over a cup of tea. Maybe I'll suggest that next time, not that I hold out much hope of her taking any notice. She's been a drinker all her adult life.

It's a pity really because she's a good-looking woman. Not pretty, not in the conventional sense, but striking. Thick blonde hair, high cheekbones and deep set eyes. It's the skin that lets her down. She's got these tiny broken spider veins all over her cheeks and that's definitely down to the drinking. I'll refuse to have one next time; keep my conscience clear.

Anyway, once she had finished blasting off about Katie disappearing and Tom having a bad day, she started on about HIM. I always think of HIM as being in capital letters because she never uses his name. I don't know the whole story, of course; we lost touch after she left the children's home and went back to her dad, and it wasn't until we bumped into one another again on a train that we got back together. Anyway, it all comes under the heading of How Life Has Treated Her So Badly, and frankly, I'm getting bored with it. I mean, I got shoved into that children's home as well and I know it was hard. No parents and a gran too ill to take care of me. But it doesn't do to go on and on about the bad times. That never got anyone anywhere.

'We've all had our fair share, Lyddy,' I told her. 'Look at me – waited twelve years for a baby, and then the one son I do get goes off in a huff at the age of eighteen and I never see him.'

Funny – she's never asked why Gareth went off. If she did, would I tell her? What would I say?

'Gareth told us he's gay and now his father won't speak to him, so he's gone off to Aberdeen to live with his partner.'

That's the truth, but could I say it? Part of me thinks that maybe it's all a mistake – youngsters go through phases, don't they, and maybe when he's a bit older he'll meet a nice girl and...

Only I know it's not true. It's not that I'm prejudiced or embarrassed; I just can't bear to think that I'll never have grandchildren.

That's the bit that hurts.

Still, I never said a word about all that, though maybe it would have done Lydia good if I had. I could have gone on about Bill's redundancy and the shortage of money as well; I could have told her about Niall, the fiancé I loved with all my heart and who died of cancer at the age of twenty-four.

But I didn't. The past does best when it's left alone, that's what I say.

In the end, I just asked her if she wanted anything at the shops and heaved a sigh of relief when she said she couldn't think of a thing.

At least that way, I don't have to go back today. I know it's mean, but she's not the woman she used to be.

She's getting to be very hard work.

TOM
Friday June 29th
10.30 a.m

I got a Smiley Face stamped on my hand by the teacher lady. You get Smiley Faces when you do something good, but I got mine for drawing the picture about Katie. I drew Katie and the black bag and the stars in the sky. I wanted to draw the silver shoes but there wasn't the proper silver colour in the pencil tin and that made me cross. My teacher came up to me when I shouted – she always does. She's nice.

'Who's that?' The teacher pointed to Katie on the paper. 'Is that Katie?'

'What is it, Tom?' she asked. 'What's wrong?'

I put my pencil where the shoes ought to go and she gave me a red crayon. I threw it on the floor.

Then she tried a blue one and a green one and an orange one, and I was just getting very angry indeed, when she gave me the glittery sparkly pen that is for special things.

She's quick, my teacher, not like some stupid people. I clapped my hands – I do that when people understand me.

That's when she gave me the Smiley Face. It must have been a very good picture.

She stuck it on the wall with sticky stuff at the back.

'This is such a good picture, Tom, that I want everyone to see it,' she said.

And then she gave me a chocolate lollipop.

It's a very good lollipop. I can make patterns on the lollipop with my tongue. I like patterns.

KATIE
Friday June 29th
2.30pm

I feel sick. I swear there is something wrong with this car; I can smell the exhaust fumes even though all the windows are closed. It's so uncomfortable; you can feel every bump and dip in the road. I wish we were in Joe's van but he says that it would be far too conspicuous.

'We don't want people gawping at all my crazy paintings,' he pointed out. 'The van is just the sort of vehicle people remember and the one thing we need is to go totally unnoticed.'

When I first arrived at Milton Keynes, I had thought for one awful moment that Joe had changed his mind, decided not to go ahead with the plan after all. I scanned the car park for his van – I even walked to the back of the bus station and looked in the Long Stay bit. Then suddenly this old heap of a car rattled to a halt at the kerbside and the passenger door swung open. I jumped back in alarm – I honestly thought some guy was accosting me – and then I realised that it was Joe.

'You haven't changed!' he hissed. 'Go into the Ladies and get out of that school uniform, like NOW!'

I must have looked startled by the tone of his voice, because he broke into a grin and wrinkled his nose at me.

'The excitement of seeing me has obviously made you lose your memory!' he teased. 'Look, I can't hang around here; I'll wait for you over by that bus shelter, OK? Now hurry!'

I sped back across the bus station concourse and into the loo, pulled off my school skirt and shirt, kicked off my trainers, and wriggled into the new jeans that Joe had bought me and this ace sweatshirt from Gap. My fingers were trembling so much that I could hardly tie my shoelaces, and when I tried to put on my lipstick I smudged it and made a right mess. But there was no time to start over again.

By the time I had dodged the traffic and found Joe's car, I was out of breath.

'Jump in!' he ordered, his eyes darting from left to right. 'Quickly!'

I clambered into the car – Joe says it's an old Ford Escort – hurled my bag onto the back seat and slammed the door.

Joe rammed the car into gear, did a rapid three-point turn and headed off in the direction of Aylesbury.

'This,' he said turning to me, 'is that start of Life with a capital L! And hey, you look cool!'

He eyed me up and down and squeezed my hand and I could have burst into song with happiness. The thought of seven whole days with Joe, days without Mum getting drunk and screaming at me, or Tom throwing a tantrum or anyone telling me that I was wasting a good brain – the whole thing is just so fantastic.

And at first the journey was really exciting. We talked about the farm and Joe told me about the people there. There's Ellie and Matt, and Cassie and a guy they call Flip because he is from the Philippines and no one can pronounce his proper name. We ate crisps and chocolate and drank the cola that Joe had brought with him and told each other stupid jokes.

But after that it got really tedious. Joe didn't want to go on the motorways and so we went across country and it seemed to me that sometimes we were going round in circles. Actually, I thought that he'd lost his way and didn't want to admit it – Alice says that guys hate to lose face.

'How much further is it?' I asked after a couple of hours. 'Sussex can't be much further, surely?'

'Not long,' Joe muttered stepping on the accelerator. 'I'm taking the long route – can't risk being spotted.'

Then I started to feel sick. I'm OK on straight roads but these were twisting and bumpy. I asked Joe to stop, but he said we couldn't risk it because a girl throwing up at the side of the road was just the sort of thing to attract the attention of passing motorists. He shoved an old Tupperware box at me and now I'm clutching it and praying that I won't start puking, because that would be so unsexy.

I've been trying to sleep, trying to take my mind off the nausea and the sour taste in my mouth and the foul smell of stale tobacco and . . .

'I didn't know you smoked!' My eyes snap open and I turn to Joe.

'I don't,' he replies. 'It's a dumb habit.'

'So how come this car stinks of smoke?' I ask.

Joe glances briefly in my direction.

'It's not mine,' he says. 'I borrowed it.'

'Who from?'

'Does it matter?' He sounds edgy.

For one awful minute, I find myself thinking that he's stolen it, but I know that's stupid of me. He's hardly going to nick a car when he's so desperate to keep away from the police, is he?

'It belongs to a mate of mine,' he says, smiling and squeezing my hand. 'I've lent him my van, he's lent me his car. Simple!'

Suddenly he stamps on the brakes and spins the steering wheel.

'Here we are!'

The car jolts off the road and down a rutted path. My bottom bounces up and down and I nearly knock myself out on the roof of the car.

'OK – get out!'

Joe flings open the driver's door and jumps out, slamming the door behind him and gesturing to me to get a move on.

I'm stiff from sitting so long and my head is swimming but I can't wait to see the farm.

Only there's nothing here. Just an expanse of fields, a small copse of beech trees and a few uninterested sheep.

Joe is already striding down the path and I struggle to catch up with him, dodging great patches of mud in an attempt to keep my trainers clean.

'Where's the farm?' I gasp, touching his arm.

Joe stares straight ahead and doesn't slacken his pace.

'We're not there yet,' he says shortly. 'Come on, up here!'

He grabs my arm and pulls me up a steep, grassy slope, covered with stinging nettles.

'There!'

I look for a building, but all I can see is a dirty old Land Rover parked on a narrow, overgrown track.

'Jump in!' Joe orders, pulling a key from the back pocket of his jeans.

'What's going on? Why are we changing cars? Joe, what are you doing?'

He doesn't reply but shoves me up into the passenger seat, kicks the front tyre, and then climbs into the driving seat.

He starts the engine and the jeep lurches forward, through the bracken and bushes and down a steep slope. I lean forward to see where we are going.

My heart misses a beat.

It's a huge quarry, gouged out of the hillside, with big patches of murky water, and vast slides of mud. The odd luminous orange road cone lies incongruously on its side. I still can't see a farm.

The Land Rover's wheels spin in the thick mud and as Joe revs the engine, it seems that he's heading away from the lane, right into the quarry.

Suddenly I'm scared.

'Joe, what's happening? Where's the farm? Where are we going?'

Joe slows the Land Rover and puts a hand on my knee. His

hands are big and square and I lay mine on top of his and feel a bit better.

'I know it's a bore, darling,' he says and my whole body shivers with delight at the word, 'but doing things this way will cover our tracks. I mean, just suppose your mother has raised the alarm, and just suppose someone, somewhere reports a guy and a girl travelling in a battered old Ford Escort...'

'I get it!' I say. 'That's dead clever.'

'We'll drive across the quarry, up the lane on the other side and join the road a few miles on,' he says looking really pleased with himself. 'And later, my mate will come back and get rid of the car and no one will be any the wiser!'

And then he stops the jeep and leans over and kisses me.

It's a long kiss and his hands wander down my body and then up again and I'm not sure whether I should pull away or see what happens next.

I'm a bit scared in case I throw up all over him, and I pull away.

'Not now,' I murmur. 'Later.'

And then suddenly wonder whether that was the right thing to say.

Joe leans towards me and whispers in my left ear.

'Yes, later,' he murmurs. 'Lots of things are going to happen to you and me later, Katie Fordyce. You just wait and see.'

Something in his voice startles me, but when I look up he is smiling down at me, his hair drooping into his eyes.

He looks adorable.

I love him so much.

I do hope Tom is all right.

LYDIA
Friday June 29th
6.15 p.m.

I hate myself. Why do I do it? Why do I drink too much and make a spectacle of myself like that in front of Katie and Tom? Well, Tom's not the problem really, bless him. Oh, I know it scares him at the time, but once I'm back to myself, he settles down and forgets all about it. But Katie doesn't. Katie never forgets.

I can't get my mind off that look she gave me this morning when I was throwing up. It was pure revulsion, as if the very sight of me, squatting down with my head halfway down the loo, left no room for anything but disgust. I can't blame the kid – I'm a mess.

'A total waste of bloody space, you are!' – that's what my dad used to shout before he belted me one round the face or kicked me downstairs. It wasn't drink with him; just sheer, unrestrained anger and hatred of me. My mum died having me and I always knew that he wished I had been the one not to survive. He couldn't even be bothered to give me a name; it was my gran who chose Lydia. All my dad ever called me was 'that brat' or 'the damned kid'.

They took me into care in the end, after Gran had her heart attack. That's where I met Grace. She was one of the big kids and she was really kind to me, right from the start. I used to cry for my dad at night, which is odd when you come to think about it. When I was with him, I was scared stiff, and when I was taken away from him, all I wanted was to hear the sound of his voice and smell the tobacco on his jacket. I guess you like what's familiar at that age. Anyway, when I was really upset, Grace used to sit on the end of my bed and tell me stories and hold my hand till I fell asleep.

My dad used to visit, of course; he'd bring me comics and chocolate and after a while they'd let him take me to the park. Sometimes I'd ask if Grace could come along because she never had visitors. Dad did try to pretend he liked being with me but I could tell he was just watching the clock, waiting till he could dump me back at The Willows and get on with his life. I used to lie in bed and vow that when I had children of my own, I would be the best mother...

Oh God, what have I done? What have I done to her? Last weekend, what I said to her – it was unforgivable. It was all true – I wasn't lying, but I should never have let it slip out like that. All these years of keeping the secret and then I almost blew it. Still, she'll think it was just me and the drink, won't she? She's bound to put it down to me just having a go at Jarvis, isn't she? Because of what he did. Jarvis had his faults, God knows he did; all those get-rich-quick schemes and head in the clouds Walter Mitty stuff; all the gambling and wasting money, and then going and doing what he did and bringing shame on us all. But I have to say, he was a good father to Katie and she loved him. She loved him more than she loved me. Most people did.

But not Tom. Tom has always loved me the best. I suppose that's because I've always been there for him, night and day. It's very wearing, I can tell you, but I reckon God had to punish me somehow for – well, for what I did all those years ago and Tom's the punishment. Not that I don't love him – I do. He needs me.

I wish I could get last weekend out of my mind. I never meant it to happen; it was just that I'd been feeling really low, so I had a few little drinks. It was when I went upstairs to the loo that I found Katie, lying on the floor of her bedroom with those photograph albums, sobbing and saying how much she missed her dad. I got all confused – thought she was talking about Him. Only, of course, she doesn't know about Him. And she must never know.

I'm going to make it up to Katie, I really am. I've cooked her favourite tea – spaghetti Bolognese. I've even made the sauce myself instead of opening a tin; she'll be impressed by that. I can hear her now: 'See, Mum,' she'll say, 'you can be an ace cook when you try.' Ace is her new word at the moment.

She's ever so late which is odd, because it's Friday and they don't have any after school activities on a Friday. Still, I suppose she's jabbering away to Alice or one of her other friends. Or maybe they've all gone into town window shopping. I don't like her hanging around the mall, but at fifteen what can you say? They all do it. I guess she's not that keen on coming home if I'm honest. Poor kid.

When she gets back, I'm going to sit her down and apologise and tell her that from now on, things are going to be different. I've said it before, but this time I really mean it. It's not as if I'm dependent on the drink – I can give it up, no trouble.

And I will this time.

I do wish Katie would hurry up. Tom's kicking up a fuss, wanting his tea. The minibus driver said that he had been in a dreadful state in the bus on the way to school, banging his head, shouting, trying to get out of his seat belt.

'Worse than I've seen him for a long time, Mrs Fordyce,' he said when he dropped Tom back. 'And the teachers say he's been restless all day.'

Perhaps he did notice more last night than I thought he did. No – not Tom. Tom doesn't take things in.

I've told him we can't eat till Katie gets back and he keeps going to the door and banging it with his fists and shouting. I did try sitting him down with his felt tips and some paper, because drawing usually settles him, but all he did was draw huge black circles all over the paper. Looked like a mass of rubbish bags, they did. That's not like him at all; it's his one major skill, art – I keep hoping that if only the speech therapist can get him to talk, he might get a little job when he's older, drawing Christmas cards or such like. You have to hope or you would go crazy.

There he goes kicking the front door again. He knows Katie is due back; he seems to sense things like that.

'She'll be back in a moment, Tom love!'

Doesn't make any difference what you tell him. He's yelling even louder now. I'd better shut the windows before the neighbours complain.

I'll get his tea and Katie can have hers later. With Tom, everything has to be routine. You can't ever do anything different, day after day.

Sometimes I wonder how I stay sane.

Oh, please come on, Katie love. Come on.

TOM
Friday June 29th
7.15 p.m.

Today's a bad day. A horrible, no-pattern messy day and I'm scared. The back-of-the-head feeling won't go away, not even with shaking and banging. Everything has stopped being like it should be and gone all fuzzy and dangerous.

Mum says Katie's coming home soon, but she's not. I know she's not. Mum says we can't eat tea till Katie comes but she won't come. I can feel it in my head. Katie said everything would be OK, but it can't be OK because the pattern's not right. She comes home for her tea. Every day. Sometimes she stays at home and sometimes she goes out again, but she always eats tea in the kitchen at the table with her orange mug with the funny face. Always.

Katie said she was going for walks with the Joe man, walks in the woods. We went to the woods once. We took sandwiches and sat on a blanket. I liked the woods; the trees made whispering sounds and the shadows on the ground danced into different patterns. Katie picked flowers and put them under my nose and they made me sneeze and everyone laughed.

Katie can't go to the woods without Mum and me.

Mum's getting angry now. She's throwing supper onto plates and banging mine down on the table.

'Right, that's it!' She pulls out my chair and points to it. I know that means I have to sit down but I can't. I sit next to Katie at teatime and Katie's not in her chair, so I can't sit in mine. It's not the right way.

'Where is she? Where can she be?' Mum's walking up and down, up and down, from the kitchen to the front door and back again, and then up and back, up and back. I don't like it. I close my eyes and rock. Forwards, back, forwards, back. Shut it out. Shut all of them out.

'Come on, Tom, sit up at the table!' Arms pulling me, but I keep my eyes tight closed.

'Time to eat tea, Tom!'

But I won't. I can't. I want Katie.

'Oh Tom, where is she?'

In the woods. She said she would be in the woods. Find the paper in the toy box, take the felt tips, draw the trees, show her. Show Mum the trees with Katie walking. But not the Joe man. He's not part of the pattern.

Show Mum the picture.

'Take it, take it!' Push her, shout louder.

'Lovely, Tom dear, lovely!'

She looked but she didn't see.

People do that a lot with me.

It makes me angry, very angry indeed.

GRACE
Friday June 29th
9.00 p.m.

My Bill wasn't best pleased, I can tell you. You can't blame him – there we were, just sitting down to our fish pie when the phone rang.

'Leave it, love,' Bill said, scooping peas onto his plate as if this was going to be his last meal.

He always says that but he knows I can't. What if it was Gareth, calling to build bridges and getting no answer? What if he'd been in an accident and Jez, his partner, was calling to tell us?

Of course it wasn't Gareth; it was Lydia.

'Can you come over?' she gabbled before I'd had the chance to even say hello. 'Now?'

'I can't, Lydia,' I began and as soon as he heard her name, Bill shook his head furiously and gestured to me to get back to the table. 'We're eating.'

'It's Katie,' she said, totally ignoring my last remark. 'She's playing me up again.'

'Lydia, dear, that's between you and Katie,' I began. 'I can't...'

'She hasn't come home,' she said.

Well, as I said to Bill, what could I do? It wasn't as if Katie was just an hour or so late home; it was nine o'clock at night, for heaven's sake.

'It's not your problem, Grace,' he muttered as I stuffed the fish pie down my throat in double quick time. 'Katie's not your responsibility.'

I told him straight then.

'It's that kind of attitude that's got this country into the mess it's in right now!' I snapped back. 'Think of number one, and let the other guy go hang!'

Bill looked a bit taken aback but I was in full flood by then. Mind you, there was no excuse for what I said next.

'You may be happy to wash your hands of your own son, but I happen to think that people matter!'

As soon as the words were out of my mouth, I regretted them. He went really pale and he pushed the food about on the plate. If he'd said something – anything – about how he missed Gareth, or how he wanted to give things another go, I'm sure I'd have sat down and that would have been that. But he didn't.

'So,' I said, pushing back my chair and standing up, 'since you've seen to it that I don't have a son to care for any more, I'll be getting over to Lydia's and try to find out what's going on with Katie.'

I had to stop halfway across the road and compose myself. I was close to tears. I try to be brave, but I do miss Gareth. Oh, I know that at nineteen, lads are rarely at home with their mothers – but at least most people have them turning up in the university holidays, or popping in at weekends. Gareth's not a bad lad; he phones me once a week; he used to ask if his dad wanted a word, but he doesn't bother any more. He knows the answer. I always make a point of asking after Jez and sending my best wishes and I think he likes that. He did invite me to go up to Aberdeen to stay but I couldn't bring myself to do that. Not while he and Jez are – well, I couldn't. I don't like myself for it, but there it is.

So I guess I'm no better than Bill really.

It was while I was thinking about Gareth and the reasons why I couldn't face going up to visit that it suddenly hit me. It was obvious where Katie was! She'd be at that sleepover party she'd been going on about – the one that Lydia refused to let her go to. I was surprised that Lydia hadn't thought of it herself.

'Now, Lyddy, don't worry, I think I know where she is!' I burst out, the instant she opened the front door. She looked in a state and I could hear Tom in the sitting room, moaning in that low monotone he adopts when he's switching off from everyone around him. 'I reckon she's gone to that party.'

Lydia stared at me.

'Party? What party?'

I couldn't believe she'd forgotten, not after all the fuss she made when Katie suggested it. But that's what drink does – it scrambles your brain.

'You remember,' I urged her, following her into the sitting room. 'She said that some friend of hers was having a sleep-over and she wanted to go. You said she couldn't because ...'

'That's right!' Recognition dawned on Lydia's face and she grabbed my arm and pulled me into the sitting room. 'And you think she's actually dared to defy me and ...'

'Well, at least if she's there, we know she's safe, don't we?' I interjected hurriedly. 'Why don't you give this girl a ring and check that Katie's there?'

The moment I had spoken Katie's name, little Tom started shouting and rocking and pulling at his hair so hard I thought he'd tear it out at the roots.

'Quiet, Tom!' Lydia put a hand on his shoulder and squatted down beside him. 'Hush!'

But he didn't look at her. He just turned away and went on rocking.

'I'll just hang on while you make the call,' I went on, 'and then I must be getting back. Have you got the number?'

Lydia frowned.

'I can't even remember the girl's name,' she confessed. 'It wasn't Alice, was it?'

I shook my head.

'Mandy,' I said. 'I remember because we once had a little Yorkshire terrier called Mandy!'

Lydia began laughing and then stopped.

'I don't know anyone called Mandy at her school,' she said. 'It must be some new girl.'

'So,' I sighed, 'you don't have a phone number?'

Lydia shook her head and began pacing up and down the room.

'When I get my hands on that girl...'

I didn't want to think about what she might do when Katie finally appeared, so I grabbed the telephone directory and shoved it into her hands.

'So phone Alice's mum!' I urged. I knew Alice was Katie's best friend; there was a time when they'd been inseparable. 'She'll know where the party is.'

You'd think I had just discovered a shortcut to the moon.

'That's a great idea!' Lydia cried, tossing the directory aside and snatching the phone. 'I know the number – I should do, what with the amount of times it appears on the phone bill. 556554!'

She punched the digits and paused.

'Engaged!' she grumbled. 'Never mind, I'll get Tom to bed and then we'll have a drink and...'

'I really can't stay, Lydia,' I interrupted. 'I've got to get back. We haven't had our pudding yet.'

To be honest, it was only sliced banana and a yoghurt but it was a good excuse to get away.

'Don't go!' She looked at me pleadingly. 'Just have a quick brandy and then...'

'No Lyddy!' As soon as I'd said it, I felt guilty. After all, her daughter was missing and she was there all on her own with Tom. The last thing I wanted was for her to start hitting the bottle once my back was turned.

'Look,' I said hastily, 'I'll pop back and get Bill his

pudding and then once you've made contact with Katie, you can give me a ring and I'll pop over for a cup of tea. How would that be?'

'OK then,' nodded Lydia. 'I'll need to calm down once I've given Katie a piece of my mind.'

I didn't doubt it. But at least if I went back, Lydia was less likely to go storming off to collect Katie from the party. Kids hate it when their mothers do that sort of thing; I know because I once dragged Gareth out of one of the more seedy discos in town and his mates teased him about it for weeks afterwards.

'Is Katie back?' Bill jumped out of his chair the moment I opened the front door and was at my side in an instant. 'Is everything OK?'

He's a good man, really. I filled him in on the story.

'She's phoning round,' I told him. 'She'll call me when she's made sure Katie's at this party.'

I haven't said I'm going back in a bit. Chances are, he'll either be up in the attic with his trains or fast asleep in front of the News. With a bit of luck, I can pop over and back without him ever knowing.

I do hope Katie's OK at that party – not mixing with the wrong sort or anything like that. You can't be too careful with youngsters these days. You never know how they're going to turn out.

Still, she's a good girl deep down, bless her. She deserves a bit of fun.

KATIE
Friday June 29th
8.10 p.m.

Joe says we're nearly there. We're going down tiny lanes with hedges either side, through little villages with funny names: Twineham, Wineham, Poynings, Fulking. Part of me is relieved that we can stop soon; I'm so tired, my eyes keep closing of their own accord. I just want to get there so that I can curl up in a ball and go to sleep. And yet, in some ways, I don't want to arrive. I'm really nervous – what if his mates don't like me? I mean, they're all his age or even older and they might think I'm just some stupid schoolkid. Joe says he's told them I'm his girlfriend – and that's dead cool and everything, but will they expect us to – well, sleep together? It's not that I don't fancy Joe – I do, a lot. But I'm scared.

Alice would probably laugh her head off if she knew what I was thinking; but then, Alice has been going out with boys since she was twelve. I've never had a boyfriend before, not a proper one. I've snogged a couple of guys at parties, but when they got to the groping bit, I backed off. I know it would be different with Joe, but I'm worried that I won't – wouldn't – know what to do. We've kissed of course – but I'm not really sure that I even get that right, because sometimes Joe will be getting really passionate and then suddenly, he pushes me away and goes all silent and grumpy on me. It's as if half of him wants to love me and the other half is annoyed because he does.

That's what happened earlier today. I guess it was probably because Joe was so uptight because of everything that had happened after we picked up the Land Rover. He had been in a really good mood when we first set off across the quarry, teasing me every time I squealed over the bumps and dips and pretending to get the jeep stuck in the mud and then spinning the tyres.

But later, after we had hit the road again and been driving for about twenty minutes, he suddenly glanced at the dashboard and exploded.

'I don't believe it!' He banged his fist onto the steering wheel and slammed on the brakes. 'Stupid bloody man! Can't he do anything right?'

'Who? What's wrong?' I asked in alarm.

'That's what's wrong,' he retorted, jabbing a finger at one of the dials on the dashboard. 'Look!'

I looked. The needle on the petrol gauge was practically on the bottom of the red line.

'Terrific!' he shouted. 'What the hell am I supposed to do now?'

'Don't worry,' I ventured. 'There's bound to be a petrol station somewhere near here.'

'Oh, sure there is!' he snapped back. 'Just like there's bound to be some smart ass cashier who is going to remember a battered Land Rover. And you can bet if the police start asking questions, he'll also remember a young girl sitting in the front and – oh, why couldn't he get this one thing right?'

He rammed the jeep into gear and headed off down the narrow winding road, clenching the steering wheel so tightly that his knuckles turned white.

'If I've told him once, I've told him a thousand times...'

'Told who what?' I asked.

'My bloody...oh nothing!' Joe snapped, and then sighed and turned to me with the glimmer of a smile. 'It's just that he – the guy I borrowed this jeep from – he was meant to fill it up before he dropped it off.'

'Oh right,' I murmured and then a thought struck me. 'This

guy – your mate – he won't go and tell, will he? I mean, you can trust him?'

Joe leaned back in his seat and roared with laughter. I was pleased that his mood had lightened, but I couldn't see what was so funny.

'Believe me,' he chuckled, 'he won't say a word. He's as dead keen for this to work out as I am.'

'What . . . ?' I began.

'Hey, don't look so worried!' he said, taking my hand. 'I had to tell him a bit about you – to explain why I needed the Land Rover. He couldn't believe what your mum had done and said he wanted to do whatever he could to help.'

He let go of my hand and manoeuvred the car round a sharp bend and onto the slip road towards the dual carriageway.

'And having got this far, we can't risk messing things up,' he continued. 'So as soon as we find a petrol station, you will have to get down on the floor and pull one of those sleeping bags over you.'

He gestured over his shoulder to the back of the jeep. I couldn't see how there was going to be room for me to perch anywhere, never mind lie down. The space at the back was crammed full of bits of wood, a pile of tow ropes, boxes of food and one of those orange and black toolboxes like Dad used to have, the one he used to let me tidy out when I was little.

For a second, I felt my eyes filling with tears. That happens when I find myself unexpectedly thinking about the past, but I didn't want Joe to think I was a wimp so I turned and stared at the passing scenery.

'Hey, look!' I grabbed Joe's sleeve and gestured out of the window. 'See that sign – "Services 4 miles".'

'Thank God!' Joe breathed, and then threw an anxious glance at the dashboard. 'Let's hope we can make it.'

As we neared the slip road to the service station, Joe

ordered me to clamber into the back and lie down behind the seats with the sleeping bag over me.

'They won't take any notice of me,' he went on, 'but if your mother has phoned the police and someone sees you ... '

He left the sentence hanging in the air.

'She won't have,' I assured him, yanking the sleeping bag over my head.

'Why? She'll be dead worried by now, surely?'

'She'll think I've gone to Mandy's party,' I explained, pulling the bag away from my mouth and shouting over the noise of the engine. 'She'll go ballistic and slam a few doors and then she'll pour a brandy and that'll be that till tomorrow morning.'

'But then she'll be in a real state, yeah?' Joe's voice wafted over to me, filled with urgency. 'She'll do the frantic mother bit, not eating, not sleeping, all that stuff?'

To be honest, I hoped she might. I mean, that's what all this is about: to get Mum to realise how much she really loves me and how much I mean to her. What I was more worried about was Tom. I knew he'd be getting really upset: anything that changes his routine terrifies him and once he's found out that I'm not there, he'd be likely to go into one of his manic moods, screaming and throwing things and refusing to eat.

'Get down!' My thoughts were interrupted by the urgency of Joe's voice. 'We're just pulling up to the fuel pumps now – oh my God!'

Before I could ask what was wrong, I was thrown against the side of the jeep, as Joe turned it round and accelerated away.

'What's going on?'

I edged my head out of the sleeping bag.

'Keep down!' Joe shouted. 'So your mother wasn't going to phone the police, is that right? So how come there was a squad car parked on the forecourt?'

For a moment, my heart lurched. They couldn't find us yet

– Mum wouldn't have had time to think about everything she had said and done to me, time to realise that she had to change. And yet, if she had called the police, it must be because she put me above everything else. I knew how she felt about police officers.

Then I realised how daft it all was. No way were the police in this corner of Sussex hunting for us.

'Police cars need petrol too,' I shouted back to Joe. 'You're not telling me that out of all the petrol stations between Hartfield and here, they just knew we were going to stop at this one? Get real!'

There was a long silence.

'And if you don't mind, I need to sit up. This sleeping bag stinks!'

'OK,' I heard Joe mutter. 'And you're probably right – I guess I overreacted. But we can't drive far – we're practically out of fuel.'

I clambered into a sitting position and peered out of the window.

'Turn down that side road,' I suggested. 'We could park up for a bit and then go back when the coast is clear.'

Joe stared at me and then nodded slowly.

'Good idea,' he agreed. 'And just to be on the safe side ... '

He didn't finish his sentence because at that moment, a burst of tinny music filled the jeep.

'Sod it!' He slammed on the brakes, leaned over to the back seat and grabbed his jacket. 'I thought I'd switched the damned thing off!'

He grabbed his mobile phone and punched the OK button.

'Yes. No, everything bloody isn't going to plan. What? I can't talk now. I'll call later.'

He punched another button and flung the phone onto the back seat.

'Who was that?'

'What? Oh – the guy who lent me the jeep. Wanted to know if everything was OK. I'll sort him later.'

He drove a little further down the side round and pulled into a layby.

'To be on the safe side, we'll leave the jeep and go for a walk. Just in case that police car has followed us. OK?'

We didn't walk far though. We clambered over a gate and wandered along a track until we came to a clump of tall gorse bushes. Joe pulled me behind them, and suddenly turned and cupped my face in his hands.

'You're really very pretty,' he whispered, tracing the line of my jaw with his finger. 'It makes it so hard...'

My body was tingling in a way I'd never known before.

'Why?' I whispered. 'Why is it hard?'

'Because I can't...'

He dropped his hand and turned away.

'Yes, you can,' I blurted out, and then wished I hadn't. I didn't know what he wanted but I had a fair idea. All I wanted was a long lingering kiss, an endless hug, his fingers running through my hair. What I didn't want was for his mood to change.

It all happened so fast. He turned back to me, took my shoulders and pulled me towards him. His lips fastened onto mine and he kissed me hard – too hard. His mouth ran down my neck and up again, and then he pushed me to the ground and sank down on his knees beside me.

'Why do you have to be so pretty?' he groaned, running his hand over my thigh. He leaned over me and kissed me again, gently this time, so gently that I relaxed and let my hands caress the back of his neck and run slowly down his body. I felt warm, loved, a woman.

And then he grabbed my arms and shoved me away.

'Stop it! Don't do this to me!'

'What? What did I do wrong?' I was close to tears.

'Nothing – everything – come on, we need to get petrol.'

He turned and strode ahead of me, back to the Land Rover. I had to go through the whole ritual of hiding under the sleeping bag again, but I didn't care. I was even prepared to put up with the smell because at least under there, I could let the tears come. Suddenly I felt homesick; I wanted to be in my own bedroom with Tom chuntering away next door. I wanted to be able to phone Alice and talk about love and boys and sex and pretend that I knew it all. I wished I hadn't come.

Of course, that feeling hasn't lasted. We got the petrol and Joe bought two cheese rolls and some Mars bars and cans of cola and we stuffed ourselves as we drove the last few miles. And now we're nearly there.

I look at Joe. He seems distracted, chewing his lip and occasionally nibbling his thumbnail. I do hope I haven't let him down, that he doesn't think I'm cold or frigid.

'This is it!'

Joe spins the steering wheel and the Land Rover jolts off the road and down a rutted track A wooden signpost points to 'Foxhole Farm', the lettering so weathered with age and mildew that it is hard to read. My heart starts to pound with a mixture of nerves and excitement.

I peer through the windscreen for a sight of the farm but all I can see is a tumbledown, single-storey cottage with boarded-up windows and grass growing out of the roof tiles.

To my amazement, Joe stops the jeep and turns off the engine.

'Out you get!' His face is shining with excitement as he leans across me and throws open the passenger door. 'We'll spend the night here.'

'But this isn't the farm!' I protest.

'I know,' he says calmly. 'But I have to check things out over there before we turn up – you know, make sure the coast is clear and all that. I'll do it in the morning. All that delay with the petrol has made us late.'

He grabs my holdall in one hand and gives me a gentle shove towards the cottage door. Kicking it open with one foot, he pulls me in and dumps the bag on the peeling linoleum.

'Joe, we can't stay here! It's awful! Just look at it!'

Cobwebs hang from the ceiling and in the gloom I can see what look horribly like mouse droppings on the faded and torn rug in the middle of the room. There's a battered sofa in one corner, its stuffing poking through the seat, and in another an old table with an oilcloth thrown over it. A single light bulb dangles from the ceiling but when I flick the switch by the door, nothing happens.

'It's only for tonight!' Joe assures me, grabbing my hand. 'Come on, let's light some candles!'

He fumbles in his jacket pocket and produces a box of matches and three candles.

'Hang on!' He runs back to the jeep and comes back with two empty Coke cans.

'These will do,' he says eagerly, jamming the candles into the cans and lighting them.

The flickering light shows up the full horror of the place.

'Joe, it's horrible!' Now I'm crying and frankly, I don't care. He can't expect me to sleep here. 'If we can't go to the farm, why don't we sleep in the Land Rover – anything would be better than here.'

'Crying won't get you anywhere!'

Joe's voice is so sharp that I actually gasp out loud.

'Sorry, darling, sorry,' he says hastily putting his arm round my shoulders. 'I didn't mean to snap – I'm tired after all the driving. But we have to be realistic – what if one of the guys at the farm has had a couple too many beers in the pub and spilt the beans about you coming? I have to take care of you.'

He kisses me lightly on the nose, takes my hand and leads me back to the door.

'And if you really want to sleep in the jeep, I guess we can,' he sighs. 'But first, I've got a surprise.'

He runs out to the jeep for a second time and comes back with one of those blue camping Gaz stoves and a cardboard box.

'Soup!' he shouts. 'And spaghetti! You told me spaghetti was your favourite thing! We'll have a picnic before we go to bed. Come on, smile!'

I know he's trying to be kind, but suddenly I'm scared.

It's silly, I know. But I don't want to go to bed with Joe.

I don't want to be here.

I just want to get to the farm and be with the other people and have a proper bed to sleep in. On my own.

Running away seemed like such a good idea a week ago. Now I'm not so sure.

'So where is the farmhouse?' I hear myself ask. Perhaps I can persuade him to take the risk and drive there now.

'Oh, not far – that way,' he says, gesturing vaguely in the direction of a clump of trees.

'So can't we...?'

'No! I've told you – I've got it all planned. You have to trust me. Come on – have a drink!'

He hands me an open can of Red Bull.

I'd rather have a Pepsi, but I don't want to look like some wet kid.

'Cool!' I smile and take a big slug of it. It's foul but I don't let on.

'So do you want to eat now?' Joe asks.

'OK,' I say. 'But first I need the loo. Where is it?'

Joe shrugs.

'Behind the nearest bush, I guess,' he mutters.

'You mean – there's no loo? Joe, I can't just...'

'Well, it's that or nothing!' Joe looks irritated. 'And hurry up about it!'

I want to go home.

It may not be great at home, but at least it's clean and I know what to expect. When things get dodgy at home, I can just shut myself in my room and let Mum get on with it.

Right now, stuck in this grotty cottage, home suddenly seems a pretty good place to be.

LYDIA
Friday June 29th
9.45 p.m.

She's so stuck up, that Alice's mother! Speaking to me as if I'd just crawled out from under a log.

'We're in the middle of a dinner party,' she chirruped when I said who it was. 'Can I phone you back tomorrow?'

'No you can't!' I snapped. OK, so I know I shouldn't have spoken like that, but I'd just had a real battle with Tom and now she wasn't letting me get a word in edgeways. 'Katie's missing!'

That got her.

'Missing?' she queried in that clipped voice of hers. 'What do you mean, missing?'

'She hasn't come home from school and I'm pretty sure she's gone to Mandy someone or other – for a sleepover party.'

'Oh, that! Yes, Alice is there but . . . '

'But what?'

'Well, Alice said something about Katie not being allowed to go. To be honest, Alice was incandescent about it – thought it was really mean of you, but of course, as I told her, it's none of our business and . . . '

'Too right it's not!' I snapped. Well, can you blame me? The wretched woman made it sound as if I was Attila the Hun.

'Anyway,' I hurried on, 'I think the little madam has defied me and gone anyway, and I need to get in touch with her. Urgently. So if you've got the phone number . . . '

'Haven't you got it?'

'If I'd got it, I wouldn't be asking you for it,' I retorted. 'So if you could . . . '

'Hang on – I'll see if I can find it.'

There was a clatter as she put the handset down and I could hear a lot of raised voices and giggling in the background.

'Katie's mum...in a state...so what's new...fancy not knowing...some mothers – always been strange!'

As if it was my fault that Katie's a deceitful, double-crossing little so and so. And I bet she'd be in a state if she'd had the life I've had. How dare she – her and her stockbroker husband, and Aga and hot tub in the conservatory.

'Right!' She was back on the phone, all breathy and triumphant. 'Mandy Russell, 18 The Birches, Frampton. The number is 01604 411324. Now I really must go – my soufflé will be ruined.'

And with that, the phone went dead.

I'll phone now and sort that little madam out. 411324. It's ringing. Come on, come on – I bet those kids have got the music blaring out and can't hear the phone.

I'll just pour myself a little drink and try again in a minute or two.

I hope she is there. I mean, I'll be furious with her, but at least I'll know she's OK. What if she's not there? What if she's had an accident?

No, I'm being silly. I must keep calm. This brandy will settle me – it always does. Just another little top-up and then I'll try that number again.

'One day, I'm going to walk out that door and never, ever come back again!'

That's what Katie said – the other day, after we'd had that awful row. What if she really has? What if she's done a bunk, just like I did all those years ago?

But no – that's silly. Kids are always threatening to run away, aren't they? And besides, where would she go? She likes her home comforts; she's not the type to go wandering the streets. She'll have gone to that party, I'm sure of it.

Oh for heaven's sake! Now there's Tom making a racket again. All evening, he's been unsettled. I tried to settle him down with his jigsaws but that didn't work and when I gave him his crayons and some paper he just drew a whole lot more dustbins and black bags all over the page.

'Draw something nice, Tom,' I told him, but of course, that was wrong and set him screaming and kicking like a thing possessed.

I'll have to give him a good dose of sedative; I can't cope with any more upheavals.

I'll just top up my glass, pop up to Tom and then I'll try that number again.

No peace for the wicked.

KATIE
Friday June 29th
10.10 p.m.

I feel better now. All mellow and very woozy. That Red Bull stuff tastes OK once you get used to it – the more you have, the better it gets. I can't believe I was such a wimp – after all, it's only for one night and as Joe says, getting caught now would be a disaster.

'Just imagine,' he said while he was heating up the soup, 'what it would be like to be dragged off back home now. Your mum wouldn't have had time to worry, she wouldn't have had to answer questions at the police station . . . she wouldn't have suffered at all. Bad mothers should be made to suffer.'

He stirred the soup so violently that it splashed over the edge of the saucepan and made the flame sizzle.

'She's not all bad,' I replied hastily. 'She's really patient with Tom. He's quite difficult and she . . . '

'I'm not interested in bloody Tom!' he shouted, and then checked himself, reached out and touched my arm. 'It's you I care about!'

'Well, she can be really nice to me sometimes.'

I don't know quite what made me leap to her defence; I just felt uncomfortable with Joe slagging her off so violently. And at that point I still felt a bit homesick.

'Oh sure! So nice that she can reject her own kid and . . . '

'She hasn't rejected me! It's just that she – well, gets drunk and says things she doesn't mean and . . . '

'And is a thoroughly bad lot!'

He slopped the hot soup into two plastic mugs and wrenched the ring-pull off the can of spaghetti.

95

I wanted to tell him that she'd only got this bad since my dad died. I sometimes think that if Dad had got ill and died in hospital or been run over by a car or something, she would have coped better. But dying the way he did...

'So what was your mum like?' I asked, blowing on my soup and trying to put all thoughts of Dad out of my mind. Joe had told me that his mother was dead but whenever I asked questions about her or anyone else in his family, he always changed the subject.

'I mean, you don't have to tell me if you don't want to but...'

Joe stared at me and then his face softened.

'My mum was pretty,' he said quietly. 'Really pretty.'

He cupped my chin in his hand and leaned towards me.

'She looked quite a bit like you, in fact,' he said softly. 'Same hair, same plump little cheeks...'

He gave one of them a friendly pinch. At least, I think it was meant to be friendly, but to be honest, it hurt.

'And did you get your odd eyes from her?' I asked, pulling back out of his reach. 'I haven't a clue where mine came from.'

I had never mentioned our eyes before – I know that when I was younger I hated mine and thought that maybe Joe felt the same.

'I didn't inherit anything from her, thank God!' he retorted, his mood suddenly changing. 'She may have been pretty but she was a cow! Having babies turned her bad!'

'What?'

'It happens,' he said, sipping his soup. 'You'll probably turn bad inside when you have babies. *If* you have them. Which hopefully you won't.'

'That's a horrible thing to say!'

I couldn't help myself; it just came out. I may be stupid, but lately I've had this silly daydream that one day Joe and I will get married and have kids. And now Joe was talking as if everyone who had children turned out to be terrible mothers.

Even me.

'Katie, I'm sorry!' He put his mug down and pulled me towards him. 'I didn't mean it!'

He sighed.

'I just get so angry when I remember everything that she did.'

'Your mum?'

'Yes – no, yours, silly. The things she did to you. The other day.'

He kissed my chin.

'Sorry,' he said again.

'It's OK,' I murmured, although to be honest I'm still a bit wary. His temper seems to flare up from nowhere, just like Mum's. Not, of course, that Joe is anything like Mum really. I guess he's just stressed out after the long day.

'Your mum died, didn't she?' I asked gently. 'What happened to her?'

Before the words were out of my mouth, I saw his face darken as he clenched his fists and turned away from me.

'She went out for a walk and she – just died.'

His voice was flat and I could see his shoulders tense.

'My dad came in the next day and sat me down and said, "Listen, boy, your mother's dead and gone and that's that".'

He bit down hard on his thumb and turned away.

'That's awful!' I murmured, touching his arm, but he shrugged me off. It was bad enough his mum dying but to hear about it like that, in such a callous way. Poor little boy.

'Yes, it is. Awful.'

He paused and then turned to face me.

'I'll get some more drinks from the jeep,' he said, his face still expressionless.

I watched as he walked slowly to the Land Rover, his hands stuffing into the pockets of his jeans. I so much wanted to run after him, and hold him and tell him that it was OK to miss his mum, and that he should talk about her – but I was

97

already feeling light-headed; my legs felt as if they were going to give way under me.

He came back a few minutes ago, and he seems more cheerful.

'There!' He hands me another bottle of Red Bull; I take a couple of gulps but I can't be bothered to drink any more. My eyes feel so heavy; I just want to sleep. I can't stop yawning.

'I'm so tired!' I can hardly speak; my tongue feels puffy and everything is going blurry.

'That's good!'

Now Joe is spreading out the sleeping bags and piling up the pillows.

'Over here!' He's beckoning me. Don't want to sleep with him but I've got to sleep. My legs feel like lead and I can hardly walk.

'I've got you!'

Joe's grabbed my arm and I feel myself being lowered onto the floor. The pillows are so soft and my head is so fuzzy.

I can't stay awake any more.

I hope Tom's asleep. I lied to him.

I wish I hadn't...

GRACE
Saturday June 30th
12.45 a.m.

It's no good, I can't sleep. I'll have to get up and make myself a hot drink otherwise I'll wake Bill with all my tossing and turning and then he'll be grumpy.

I should have insisted. I know I should. I should have made Lydia telephone the police. You would think she would have wanted to; Katie's only fifteen and you can't be too careful.

'Did you phone that Mandy girl?' I asked her when I popped back. 'Is everything OK?'

Lydia shook her head.

'I've had my hands full with Tom,' she said. 'I've only just got him off to sleep and that took a double dose of sedative.'

I could tell by the way she was weaving down the hall towards the kitchen that she'd had a double dose of something – and I had a fair idea what it was.

'Drink?' She turned and smiled hazily at me.

'I'll have a cup of tea,' I replied firmly. 'But first you are going to make that phone call.'

I marched over to the phone, grabbed the handset and thrust it into her hand.

'OK, OK,' she sighed, punched in the numbers and stood, drumming her fingers on the sideboard.

'No reply!' She banged the receiver down.

'But there must be!' I protested. 'I mean, if they're having a party...'

'Music!' replied Lydia, unscrewing the top of the brandy bottle. 'You clearly don't know much about teenagers.'

That cut deep, but I shrugged it off.

'But the parents,' I went on, 'surely they'd answer the phone?'

'Out probably,' replied Lydia.

'Out!' I couldn't help myself. 'Out – what kind of parents go out while a crowd of teenagers are in the house?'

Lydia shrugged.

'Not everyone is as caring a mother as me,' she sighed. 'Still, there's no point fretting. Mind you, I'll give her a piece of my mind in the morning.'

I tried to reason with her but she seemed quite laid back about it all. I guess that was the drink; they say it blurs the edges of your powers of reason.

I had a cup of tea, and she had one too. Trouble is, she poured the brandy into hers.

Now I can't sleep for worrying about Katie. What if she's gone off to some nightclub with her mates? What if someone's handing out drugs and she's . . . ?

Stop it, Grace, you silly old fool. You're letting your imagination run away with you. Drink your chocolate and get back to bed.

As Bill says, it's not your problem.

You can't help worrying, though. She's a nice kid, Katie, but then again, you never can tell these days.

LYDIA
Saturday June 30th
12.00 noon

She's gone. Oh my God, she's gone.

She's done it.

She's run away.

And it's all my fault.

I've got to keep calm, think this through.

Work out how to play it.

I need a drink but Grace says coffee will do and I don't have the strength to argue.

When the phone rang this morning while I was clearing away the breakfast things, I fully expected it to be Katie. I was so sure that I snatched up the phone and really let rip.

'And where the hell do you think you've been all night, young lady? How dare you defy me? You'll pay for this, Katie Fordyce!'

'It's not Katie, Mrs Fordyce; it's Alice. Isn't Katie there?'

'No she's not! I suppose she's still at that Mandy's house ...'

'She can't be. She wasn't at the party!' Alice interrupted.

That's when I started to feel sick.

'Not there?' I clutched onto the hall table for support.

'No,' affirmed Alice. 'She told me on Thursday that you wouldn't let her come, and then when she wasn't at school yesterday...'

I felt the floor sway beneath my feet.

'Not at school? Katie wasn't at school yesterday?'

'So she's not ill? I mean, I thought...'

'OH MY GOD!' It was a few seconds before I realised that

it was me who was screaming. I slammed the handset down and sank down onto the bottom stair.

'Katie, Katie! Where are you?'

I was shaking like a leaf and I couldn't stop crying.

Needless to say, that set Tom off. He came out of the kitchen, moaning and wailing and began tugging at my sleeve, his little face all screwed up with fear.

'It's OK, Tom,' I said automatically, staggering to my feet and ushering him back to the kitchen table. 'It's going to be fine. We'll find Katie.'

With that, he goes charging across the kitchen and begins yanking open the cupboard door under the sink, hurling things onto the floor – dusters and cans of polish, the dustpan, a bucket, the lot. Normally I would have tried to make it all into a game, get him to put stuff back; but I couldn't be bothered. I did try to pull him away but he just lashed out and started kicking and screaming, so I let him get on with it.

I didn't know what to do. I phoned that Mandy girl again, and got through this time, but she didn't have a clue where Katie might be. I rang the hospital, thinking that maybe she'd had an accident, but that drew a blank too.

That was when Grace phoned.

'Just thought I'd check to see Katie was back and . . .'

As soon as I heard her voice, and not Katie's, I broke down and that's when she came over.

She's still here now, taking forever to produce one cup of coffee. I said I needed something stronger, but she got quite shirty and I don't have the energy to argue. I've got my hands full just keeping Tom quiet. He's sitting on the floor beside me, rocking backwards and forwards, clutching this great roll of black bin bags. Once he had found those in the cupboard, he lost interest in the rest of the stuff, and Grace was able to clear the place up a bit. He keeps thrusting them under my nose and banging my knee with his fist. What I'm supposed to do, heaven knows.

Grace has spent the last hour or so telling me that I have to ring the police. She says that if I don't, she will, and what is that going to look like?

She's given me ten minutes to pluck up the courage. I can't face it, not again. I can't face all the questions and the veiled comments and the looks. I went through all that when Jarvis died; squad cars parked outside at all hours and that orange tape sealing the place off.

Not of course, that we'll have that this time. It's not as if Katie's dead...

Oh God.

Not that. Please, dear God, not that.

I grab the phone, punch in the number of the police station, and wait. My mouth's so dry that I doubt I'll be able speak.

Dear God, bring her back. Keep her safe.

I love her. I may be a bad mother but I do love her.

'I want to report a missing person. My daughter.'

I can hardly force the words out.

They want to know her name.

'Katie. My Katie. She's only fifteen. Find her. Please, please FIND HER!'

They're asking all sorts of stuff but all I can do is yell.

'What does it matter how long? Just find her, damn you! Find her!'

KATIE
Saturday June 30th
3.30 p.m.

This is all so weird. It's not a bit like I imagined it would be. Joe says I'm just jumpy and need to chill out and I guess he's right. After all, didn't I say that being away from home for a whole week would be like heaven on earth? So why do I feel so edgy?

Waking up the way I did this morning didn't help. I had this awful dream about Dad. Not Dad when he was alive but Dad when we found him. Slumped in a heap, his face all grey and puffy. In my dream, I could even smell the stench. Then suddenly, Dad's eyes snapped open and he stared at me. That's when I woke up screaming – and there they were. Two eyes, only centimetres from my face staring at me.

'I've got you!'

The voice wasn't Dad's.

'This time, I've really got you!'

It took a few seconds for my brain to register that these weren't Dad's eyes either; they were odd coloured, one greeny blue and the other grey, framed in sandy lashes.

My brain snapped into action. Joe.

'You were dreaming,' he said as I struggled to sit up, my heart hammering in my chest. He gently flicked my hair out of my eyes.

'It was horrible,' I stammered, my heart still racing. 'I dreamed about my dad. When he died.'

Joe sat down beside me and took my hand.

'Tell me about it,' he asked eagerly. 'You've never told me much – just that you found him dead one day. So what killed him? Did he suffer?'

104

I knew I couldn't answer. I could feel this great wad of tears rising up from the pit of my stomach and lodging somewhere around my larynx. Alice says that if there is one thing guys cannot stand, it's girls who cry in front of them. As long as I didn't speak, I knew I could control it. So I just shrugged and turned away.

'Go on, I want to know!' Joe leaned forward, tapping my arm to attract my attention. 'Was it a heart attack? An accident? A stroke?'

I wish.

I wish my father had died like other people's relatives die. In bed with clean white sheets and a vase of flowers on the table, or even suddenly, dropping like a swatted fly on the pavement with anxious onlookers clustered round, phoning for an ambulance.

No one should die like my dad.

It isn't fair.

'Katie, tell me!'

I couldn't understand why Joe was so eager, why he couldn't leave it alone. And frankly, I didn't feel like talking about it – in fact, I didn't feel much like talking at all. My mouth was dry and my tongue felt as if it had swelled to twice its normal size overnight. My head ached and I felt slightly sick.

'I'll tell you later,' I replied. 'I feel awful – I'm so thirsty. What's the time?'

'Eleven o'clock!' replied Joe. 'You slept for ages. It worked!'

'What worked?'

He grinned.

'The soporific effects of my special Red Bull cocktail,' he laughed. 'I spiked it with vodka!'

I was about to protest but thought that would only make me sound like a party pooper.

'Oh. Right.'

Joe laughed.

105

'Don't worry, I'll get you a drink. A soft one, this time!'

If this was what a hangover felt like, I thought, I was never, ever going to drink again. I couldn't imagine why Mum drank if she felt half as groggy as this every morning.

Joe pushed open the cottage door to get some more cans of drink from the Land Rover and a blast of gloriously fresh air flooded the cottage and filled my nostrils. I took great gulps of it, as shafts of sunlight cut through the dim gloom of the cottage causing me, just for a moment to close my eyes against the bright light. But only for a moment; seconds later, the smell of rain-washed grass and the sound of birds singing and a horse whinnying in the distance had me jumping to my feet and running to the door. My legs felt weak and wobbly and I had to grab onto the door frame for support, but at least my head began to clear.

'Get back inside!' Joe virtually shoved me into the darkness, thrusting a can of Dr Pepper into my hand. 'Are you crazy? Do you want the whole world to see you?'

He slammed the cottage door, shutting out all the sunlight and plunging the room back into shadowy gloom. That's when I snapped.

'For God's sake, Joe,' I shouted, ripping off the ring-pull from the can, 'who is there to see anything? It's not exactly as if there are hordes of people tramping around outside, is it? We're in the middle of nowhere, miles from the main road.'

I took several long gulps from the can. I loathe Dr Pepper but I was too thirsty to find out whether there was anything else in the jeep.

'We can't take any risks . . . ' Joe began.

'Fine! In that case, we'd better stay here for ever, hadn't we? We couldn't possibly leave for the farm, could we? I mean, we might pass someone on the way and that would never do, would it?'

I guess I did go a bit over the top but to be honest, I hate being cooped up at the best of times, never mind in a grot hole like the cottage with the remnants of that awful nightmare still floating around in my head.

'You're right!' The corners of Joe's mouth twitched, but it wasn't a smile. It was a pitying sort of leer. 'We won't be going anywhere.'

'What? I didn't mean…Joe, I'm sorry, I was just…'

I tried desperately to back pedal.

'You don't get it, do you?' Joe stared at me, a small smile tweaking the corner of his mouth. 'You are so…'

His voice tailed off.

'So what?'

Joe gave a little laugh.

'Naive,' he said. 'Trusting.'

His finger caressed my left cheek, but something in the way he looked at me made my stomach churn.

'So why wouldn't I trust you?' I asked, stepping a little nearer to him and running my tongue along my lower lip, because Alice had once said that if you're arguing with a boy, doing that is a sure way of softening them up.

'No reason at all,' he said and pulled me towards him. What happened next was the longest, slowest kiss we'd ever had and Joe didn't end it by pushing me away as he usually did.

'Oh Katie, Katie, why do you have to be so lovely?'

He pressed his lips against mine once again and my whole body felt as if it was about to melt. Then, just as suddenly as he had started, he pulled away, running his fingers through his hair and breathing heavily.

'Let's go for a walk,' he said, avoiding my eyes. 'You're right – if we stick to the woods, we'll be out of sight.'

'Why can't we just head for the farm right now?' I asked as Joe grabbed his jacket, kicked open the door and led me outside. 'I can't wait to meet your mates.'

'No!' he snapped back, so sharply that I actually jumped. He grabbed my hand and began dragging me along a narrow little path at the back of the cottage towards a clump of trees. 'Now that you're mine, I want you to myself. For a while, at least.'

I stopped and looked up at him, hardly daring to repeat his words in case I broke the spell.

'Am I really yours? For always?'

Alice would have been furious; she always says that you have to play hard to get if you want a guy to stay interested.

Joe's gaze was so intense that I felt my whole body grow hot as I held my breath, waiting for his reply.

'Katie Fordyce,' he said slowly in that deep, drawling voice of his. 'You will be mine for the rest of your life. Until the day you die.'

I guess it was because I was still basking in the warmth of those words that I didn't argue when he started asking questions about Dad again. We'd reached a little copse of trees and were lying down on the ground, gazing up through the leaves to the blue, cloud-speckled sky above. He was holding my hand and fiddling with my hair. It was so peaceful; birds were singing and it was so quiet that you could almost hear each individual leaf rustling in the breeze.

'So come on, tell me about your dad,' Joe urged, taking my hand. 'How did he die?'

I took a deep breath; after all, I told myself, if we're going to spend the rest of our lives together, he has a right to know everything.

'He killed himself,' I whispered and then I burst into tears.

'What? He topped himself? I don't believe it!'

He didn't looked shocked or disgusted like most of our friends had at the time. That was what was so weird. His expression was like someone who had expected to win five pounds and suddenly discovered it was five hundred. I thought – I hoped – that he would hold me, comfort me, but he didn't. All he did was clamber to his feet, dust the leaves off his jeans and walk to the edge of the copse.

'He did himself in! So that explains it!' I heard him mutter. I suppose it had suddenly hit him that the only reason I had been reluctant to talk about it was because of the stigma about suicide. Some of my so-called mates at school were really horrid when it happened, asking if it was something I'd done that had driven my father to kill himself. Others said that he was probably a criminal who knew he'd be caught one day and took the coward's way out. They were all wrong, but it didn't make things any easier.

Joe has been standing over there at the edge of the copse for ages, gazing into the distance while I've been struggling to stop crying and blot out the memory of those awful days after we found Dad in the garage.

I'll go over to him – perhaps he thinks I want to be on my own. If I go over he'll hug me and hold me and right now that's all I want.

As I clamber to my feet, he suddenly moves. He's pulling his mobile phone from his jacket and tossing it from hand to hand. Perhaps he's going to phone the farm and check that everything's OK. I hope so – I really want to get there and have a shower and meet everyone. He punches in a number and begins to speak.

'Listen, I've just found out ... '

Suddenly he spots me moving towards him, stops speaking and stuffs the phone back into his pocket. He turns and comes towards me, arms open.

'So why did he kill himself?' he asks, just as if there had never been a pause in the conversation.

'I didn't think you were interested!' I snap. 'You just walked off ... '

'I'm sorry, sweetheart,' he replies, touching my arm. 'I was just – well, I had to get my head around it. Your dad actually taking his own life and everything. I mean...'

His voice tailed off.

'It's OK!' I don't want him to feel bad about being embarrassed. I can't blame him. Suicide isn't the sort of thing people ever get used to talking about.

'Was he mentally ill?' Joe asks as we wander along the path back to the cottage. 'Was he dying of something awful and wanted to speed things up?'

I shake my head.

'No one knows, not for sure. But I've got a pretty good idea.'

'You have?'

I nod.

'I think it was all down to my mum,' I mutter, my voice cracking again. 'She drove him to it – there was this note...'

I can't go on. I suddenly feel as if I am betraying my dad by talking about what had happened.

'We don't wash our dirty linen in public,' he used to say to me when Mum had one of her mood crashes and yelled so loudly that the neighbours started asking questions. 'It's our business and no one else's.'

'What note? Tell me!' Joe urges, grabbing my arm. 'I mean – if it would help.'

'He'd scribbled on a post-it note and stuck it on the dashboard of his car.'

I can see it now, that lurid pink square of paper, lying incongruously so close to his slumped, still body.

'It just said, "*I did my best but it was never going to be enough. Now there's nothing more to give; it's all gone. But at least Katie will be OK*."' I recite the words flatly, trying not to think too much about what they meant.

Joe's eyes widen.

'What did he mean? "*Katie will be OK?*" Was the man some sort of idiot? Didn't he know what your mother was

110

like? Couldn't the fool see she was an evil bitch?'

His pace quickens and he strides up to the cottage door and pushes it open with a clenched fist.

'Don't you call my father a fool!' I shout, running to catch up with him. 'I'm sure he meant that he had paid my school fees in advance so that whatever happened, I wouldn't have to leave Pipers Court. That shows how much he loved me – whatever my mother might say!'

Joe shrugs.

'Was that it? I mean, was there anything else in the note?'

His face is so close to mine that I can feel the heat of his breath.

'No.'

There wasn't. It didn't say, 'Tell Katie I love her' and it didn't say 'Tell Katie I'm sorry for leaving her.'

Perhaps Mum was right after all.

Perhaps Dad didn't love me.

I can't think about that.

'So,' Joe murmurs, so softly that I can hardly hear him. 'She wrecked three lives, then, that mother of yours.'

I wipe my eyes and look up at him, trying to follow what he's saying.

'What do you mean, three lives?'

Joe's face reddens and he looks embarrassed.

'Well, I mean – your life, your dad's and ... well, Tom's, I guess. God, I hate her!'

I don't say anything. I'm too busy wondering whether I did the right thing, running off the way I did. I know Mum said some awful things, but at the end of the day, she is my mother and she is sick and perhaps I should have stayed put and made her see a doctor.

And there's something else. Joe scares me a bit. Quite a lot, some of the time. He has these awful outbursts of anger and sometimes he looks at me in a spooky kind of way, as if

111

he knows something I don't and he's really chuffed about it.

'Can we go to the farm now?' I ask. 'Is it all clear?'

I reckon that once we are there with all his mates, he'll relax and chill out.

'What?'

He looks distracted.

'When you phoned just now, did they say it was all clear?' I persisted.

'Oh – I don't know – I lost the signal!'

'Can't we just risk it anyway?' I urge him. 'It's only a couple of miles away, after all.'

Joe nods.

'OK,' he says. 'But there's something I need to get from the car. You go in and start packing up the sleeping bags.'

I don't need asking twice. I shall be so glad to get out of this place and wash off the musty smell and the grime. I can hear Joe whistling as he fumbles around in the back of the jeep; I guess he's as keen to get to the farm as I am.

'Right!' I say cheerfully to Joe as I dump the sleeping bags in the back of the Land Rover and turn back to fetch the rest of our stuff. 'I'll just get the pillows and then can we please get going?'

'We can't – I can!'

I wheel round to stare at him. He's following close behind me, and he's carrying the plastic tool kit and one of those cordless screwdrivers, the kind that Mr Whelan uses in CDT. For some reason, my heart starts beating at twice its normal speed.

'You have to stay here, while I check things out!'

He dumps the toolbox and the screwdriver on the ground and kicks open the cottage door.

'But I'm starving and . . .'

'I couldn't give a ****!'

He grabs my wrists. He's pushing me. Pushing me hard. So hard that I stumble across the floor and fall in a heap by the table.

I scream in terror.

'Joe! What are you . . . ?'

'Shut up and listen! I've got something to tell you!'

He grabs his jacket from the back of the chair and starts fumbling around in the pockets.

'Damn! Damn, damn, damn!'

He hurls the jacket to the floor.

'What is it?' I scramble to my feet. I'm really scared now.

'There's something I have to show you! Something you've got to see! And I've left it behind.'

'It doesn't matter, we . . .'

'It matters, OK?' He spits the words at me, shoving me across the room as he speaks. 'If I say it matters, it matters!'

Before I have time to regain my balance, he is out of the door.

It slams behind him.

I catch my breath.

'Joe! What are you . . . ?'

My voice is drowned by a sudden whirring drilling sound.

Instinctively I run to the window but of course, they're boarded-up and I can't see a thing.

I beat on the door with my fists.

'Joe! What the hell are you doing? JOE!'

I grab the door latch and try to pull it open. It won't budge.

Then suddenly the whirring stops and there is a clatter of falling tools.

'You can't get out so you might as well stop trying!'

'No – Joe – come back . . . don't leave me!'

My breath is coming in short gasps and I can hardly speak. My chest feels as if someone is pulling a metal band round it.

'I'll be back, silly!' Suddenly he sounds friendly again. 'But it's got to look as if this place is deserted, hasn't it? See you later!'

'Joe, wait!' I've got to sound calm. I mustn't make him angry again. 'Look, you're right, of course, but you don't need to shut me in. I'll lie low, I promise. I won't let anyone see me. Please don't leave me . . . '

'Why not?' He's shouting again now. 'People get left all the time. At least I'm coming back which is more than some people do!'

He's going. I hear him slam the door of the Land Rover, switch on the ignition, rev up the engine. There's a crashing of gears, a screeching of tyres and he's gone.

I feel sick. My knee is throbbing from where I fell and it feels as if the gloom of the cottage is closing in on me. It's very quiet. Birds are singing and there's a rustling of a branch against one of the boarded-up windows.

And no one knows I'm here.

'Help me! Help!'

My own voice sounds pathetically small and ineffectual.

My heart is pounding in my ears and I need the loo.

Keep calm. He's coming back. He said so.

The farm's not far away. He'll check it out and then he will come straight back and we'll be together.

But I don't want to be with him any more.

I don't think I even love him any more.

I want to go home.

I want my mum.

It wasn't meant to be like this.

114

TOM
Saturday June 30th
3.45 p.m.

I don't like this. I don't like these people in my house. They've been here a long time and I want them to go now.

The pattern is all wrong – there's a man sitting where Katie sits and the lady is in Mum's chair. And Mum is crying. She cries when Katie is bad, so that means these people are bad. They came once before and took my dad away. Taking things is very bad. I know it was these people because I remember the patterns on their hats. Nice patterns on very bad people.

Now the lady with the striped pencil is talking about Katie and writing things down on a pad with twirly edges.

'Has she ever run away from home before? Is there anywhere she might have gone?'

Mum shakes her head. That means no.

I shout at them. I know where she's gone. She's gone with the Joe man to the woods. Or was it the farm? Foxes on a farm.

They don't listen. They don't even look at me.

The man leans forward and stares at Mum.

'Was there a boyfriend, Mrs Fordyce? Was she seeing anyone?'

'No – she's not that type!' Mum jumps to her feet and begins walking up and down, up and down.

I shout louder and grab her leg as she goes past me.

She's with the Joe man!

'Tom, quiet!' Mum's cross. Her face is red and her eyes are wet. She picks up some paper and my felt tip pens from the table and dumps them at my feet.

'Sit nicely and draw, Tom, there's a good boy.'

She looks up at the police lady.

'He misses Katie, bless him,' she says. Her voice goes quiet, the way it always does when she talks to other people about me. The police lady nods and makes 'aah' and 'oh dear' noises.

'He doesn't understand what's happened,' Mum says.

I do understand. You're the ones who don't. Can't you see?

They go on talking. Words, words, words, up and down, louder, then softer. Things I don't understand and some I do.

'Young girls ... several incidents this summer ... dangerous ... take very seriously.'

Grace jumps up, grabbing teacups, stomping round the room.

'So what are you going to DO?'

She shouts the last word and everyone looks up. Grace isn't a shouting sort of person; Grace is a 'there, there, Tom, it's all OK' person, with a big lap and lots of songs.

'Sitting here won't find Katie!' Her voice is getting louder and louder. 'Anything could be happening to her – what if someone's taken her ... ?'

I shout that Joe's taken her to the farm but no one takes any notice.

Then the police lady starts talking.

'We need a photograph ... description of her clothes ... is anything missing?'

The black bag. That's missing. Katie put it outside but when the minibus man came the bag had gone.

It's no good telling them. They don't understand. So I draw.

I draw, fast, faster, faster – Katie with the black rubbish bag, Katie in the red pyjamas.

'That's a nice picture!' The police lady is kneeling beside me, touching my paper. 'Really lovely!'

I shout at her. It's not lovely, can't she see? It's awful. It's Katie doing a wrong thing. And now the bag is missing.

'What's that?'

She points to the black bag.

I poke her and shout. Push her arm to make her look round to where I've put the black bags by the window.

She smiles and pats my head. Then she gets up and goes to sit by Mum.

She's making me very angry.

Very angry indeed.

GRACE
Saturday June 30th
5.00 p.m.

I knew I should have done something sooner. If anything has happened to Katie, I'll never forgive myself. Bill says I've nothing to reproach myself for, but I can't help wondering whether, if only I'd made Lydia phone the police sooner... but it's too late now.

I just pray it's not too late for Katie.

It's been an awful afternoon. After my little outburst, the policewoman and the sergeant made Lydia take them to Katie's bedroom and check through all her clothes. They said that if they knew what she had taken with her, it would help them with their inquiries. They weren't up there for very long; I'd only just had time to make Tom a hot blackcurrant in an attempt to calm him down. When they came down I could tell from the look on Lydia's face that something was very wrong.

'You are absolutely sure that none of her clothes have gone?'

The policewoman laid an arm gently on Lyddy's shoulder. Lyddy nodded dumbly.

'Just the school uniform she was wearing yesterday morning,' she murmured.

'In view of that,' interjected the sergeant, rubbing his chin and avoiding Lydia's stricken gaze, 'I think we have to deduce that Katie never meant to go anywhere.'

'You mean...?'

The colour drained from Lydia's face. I felt sick.

'She may have been taken against her will,' the policewoman said softly. 'We will launch a full scale search immediately.'

Lydia was brave, I'll give her that. She swallowed hard, bit her lip and nodded.

'So – you said you'd be wanting a photo of Katie?' she asked, crossing over to the little walnut bureau in the corner of the sitting room.

'Please,' nodded the policewoman. 'And a description of her school uniform.'

'Grey skirt, white blouse, maroon sweatshirt, grey blazer with a maroon badge, and black lace-up...' Lydia paused, frowning.

'You've remembered something?' The sergeant looked up from his notebook.

'Her school shoes were upstairs beside the bed,' answered Lydia. 'But those wretched trainers – they'd gone! She actually defied me and wore her trainers to school!'

Then her face fell.

'Only she never got to school, did she?'

No one replied.

'These trainers,' asked the police sergeant. 'What were they like?'

'Hideous!' retorted Lydia. 'Silver with little studs down both sides. I would never have let her buy them only...'

'That's good!' interrupted the policewoman eagerly. 'Very distinctive. People might just remember unusual footwear like that.'

Please, I prayed silently to myself, please let someone remember them. Lydia pulled a photograph from the desk drawer and handed it to the sergeant.

'That was taken at Easter,' she said. 'Her hair's a bit longer now.'

'Unusual eyes,' remarked the policewoman, peering over the sergeant's shoulder. 'That might help. I wouldn't think you'd forget eyes like that.'

'You don't,' agreed Lydia.

It was an odd reply, but then she's been through a lot, poor lass.

'We'll get this copied and made into posters,' the policewoman explained. 'And we'll put out bulletins on the radio, TV, that sort of thing.'

She patted Lydia's arm.

'We'll find her, you'll see!' she smiled.

Please God.

They left soon after that. They've asked Lydia to phone anyone and everyone she can think of who might have a clue as to where Katie has gone. She's on the phone now and I must admit, she's holding up very well. I don't know how she does it: when my Gareth stormed off after that row with his father, I fell apart – and I knew exactly where he'd gone.

I'd better get back to Bill. Getting his tea will give me something to do.

It's the waiting that gets to you.

Saturday June 30th
10.17 p.m.

*'Good evening. This is BBC Look East with the late evening
news for the Eastern Counties. Police in the region have
launched a search throughout the East Midlands for
teenager Katie Fordyce from Hartfield. Katie, who is fifteen,
failed to turn up at school on Friday morning. In view of the
recent spate of attacks on young girls in our region, the
police are taking Katie's disappearance very seriously.
Katie is five foot three inches tall, has ash blonde hair,
freckles and eyes of differing colours, the left being green
and the right grey. She was last seen wearing her maroon
and grey Pipers Court school uniform and a pair of
distinctive silver trainers. Police are asking anyone who has
any information to contact them on 01604 567345.'*

LYDIA
Saturday June 30th
10.30 p.m.

She'll be all right. She has to be. She's done this because of
me, because of the way I drink. Of course, I didn't tell the
police that although it's sure to be on their records
somewhere that I had been drinking a bit when they found
Jarvis. 'Out of your head,' was how Katie put it at the time
but then kids do exaggerate, don't they?

I really thought at first that she'd done a bunk because I
said she couldn't go to the party. When I heard she had never

turned up at Mandy's house, I knew it was something else. I don't think anyone's taken her; she's too streetwise for that, and besides, I gave her a personal alarm when we moved here and . . .

Oh God. The alarm's still here, on the hall table. She didn't take it.

The stupid, stupid girl! How can she be so . . . ?

Oh Katie, Katie. If you come back safely, I'll never drink again. I promise. I won't shout and I'll get my act together and I'll be a good mum. I really will.

Do you hear me, God? I promise.

KATIE
Saturday June 30th
10.35 p.m.

He's not coming back. He's left me here to die. I can't get out of the door – he's screwed it shut.

I saw a mouse. It made me scream.

No one will hear me scream.

Not ever.

My head's spinning. I feel faint. There's nothing here – no knives, no scissors, no hammer. Nothing to help me get out.

I'm so hungry.

I'm so scared.

Mum will be scared too. She will have phoned the police. They'll come, won't they?

But how will they know where to start looking?

No one knows about Joe.

No one knows about the farm.

Only Tom.

And Tom can't tell a soul.

I'm going to die.

GRACE
Sunday July 1st
3.00 a.m.

I can't sleep. Every time I close my eyes I see Katie's face. Seeing her picture on the telly like that really hit home. You see these missing person appeals so often but you never expect it to happen to someone you love.

I do love Katie. I've known her since she was born. It's funny how things turn out – if I hadn't taken the day off work that Friday, I might never have met up with Lydia again. It was such a coincidence – or perhaps it was fate. Perhaps God knew that Lydia needed all the friends she could get, I don't know. I'd been down in Brighton that day, visiting an old friend, and I'd only just managed to catch the train by the skin of my teeth. It was packed, and I had to push my way through several carriages before I found a seat. When I did spot a spare one I slumped down, still gasping for breath. The woman in the seat next to me was gazing out of the window, her chin in her hands and it wasn't until we'd got as far as Preston Park station that I realised she was crying. She wasn't making a noise; I just saw her shoulders heaving and spotted a crumpled tissue screwed up in her hand.

'Are you all right, love?' I asked. It was pretty obvious that she was far from all right, but I couldn't think of anything else to say.

She didn't respond so I touched her arm, and with that, she jumped out of her skin.

'It's OK,' I said hastily, 'I just wondered if you were . . . '

The words died on my tongue. I couldn't believe my eyes.

'It's not . . . It can't be . . . '

I hesitated. The hair was a tacky sort of bright orange, which wasn't right, but there was no mistaking that snub nose and dimpled chin.

'Lyddy?'

She had already turned away, clearly embarrassed by her puffy eyes and red nose, but at the mention of her nickname, she swung back to face me.

'How do you . . . ?' She paused, staring at me, and you could almost see the years rewinding in her memory. 'Grace?'

I nodded, unable to speak and threw my arms round her

124

neck. I guess it was the wrong thing to do on a crowded train, because the moment I hugged her, she broke down again in sobs. A few people turned to stare, but I gave them one of my withering looks – the kind that Bill says would stop an invading army in its tracks and they stuck their heads back in their newspapers.

'It's so good to see you again!' I told her. 'But what is it? What's wrong?'

'Nothing, I'm fine!' she insisted, but she didn't meet my gaze.

'Oh, sure you're fine!' I retorted. 'That's what you always used to say when you were little and I never believed a word of it then!'

Her eyes filled with tears again and that's when it all poured out. To be honest, she was in such a state, and whispering so softly because of all the wagging ears around us, that I didn't catch it all myself, but there was something about a guy she'd taken up with who had got violent, and pushed her down the stairs, and how she was running away because she was scared stiff of him. I asked where she was going and she said she'd got a friend who'd offered to take her in till she got herself sorted.

'I get off here!' she said, suddenly jumping to her feet as the train pulled into Haywards Heath station. She pulled a battered holdall from the overhead rack, and began pushing past me.

'Hang on!' I said, grabbing her arm. 'You can't just reappear in my life and then vanish without trace! Where can I contact you?'

She hesitated.

'Um...I haven't got the exact address,' she mumbled. 'Give me your number and I'll call you.'

I scribbled it down on the back of an envelope and gave her another hug.

'It's so good to see you again, Lyddy,' I said.

'Is it?' She looked surprised. 'Is it really?'

I nodded.

'Thanks,' she murmured with just a trace of a smile. 'That's so nice of you.'

And with that, she pushed her way down the aisle and out of the train.

As the train pulled out of the station I saw her running up to a tall, athletic-looking guy, who snatched her up into his arms and swung her round and round, smothering her face with kisses.

I remember hoping and praying that this friend – who was clearly a lot more than that – would treat her better than the last one. Of course, I didn't know then that it was Jarvis – I didn't realise that until I was invited to the wedding. She didn't waste any time; they married just six weeks later and then the following August, I got a phone call saying that little Katie Josephine had arrived and would I be godmother? Of course I said I would, and I never mentioned to them that I was good at sums and could work out quite well that Lydia must have been pregnant before the wedding. She liked to say that Katie was premature and I went along with it. Jarvis seemed like a good man and that was enough for me.

I loved that baby the moment I set eyes on her and I've loved her ever since. I was thrilled when they finally decided to move up here a few years back, which was probably wrong of me considering it was Lydia's illness that brought it about. But it was lovely seeing more of Katie, and being able to help out with poor Tom.

If anything has happened to that darling girl...

TOM
Sunday July 1st
4.30 a.m.

She's here! She's come home! I was dreaming she was here, and now I've opened my eyes and there she is, at the end of my bed, and there are tears running down her face.

I throw back the covers and jump out of bed.

'Katie!'

I open my arms for a hug and throw myself at her.

I fall bang on the floor.

Katie's not there. The room is empty. There's no one here.

In my head I saw her. She was telling me about the Joe man and the farm but she wasn't smiling. She was crying.

She was calling my name, over and over again.

'Tom! Oh, Tom!'

The bad feeling in the back of my head is starting. Katie's not here because bad things are happening to her.

I know they are.

I bang my fists against my head to kill the feeling but it won't go.

KATIE! KATIE!

Bits of the dream keep coming into my head. There's Katie in a car with Joe man. She told me about Joe man's car, how it had flowers painted on it.

It didn't have flowers in my dream.

It was dirty and Katie was crying.

KATIE!

Now Mum's come and she's putting me back in bed.

'It's OK, Tom, it was just a bad dream!'

I hit her with my hands, I push her, I bang her, I try to tell her that something bad is happening, but she just goes into the bathroom and brings back the bottle of purple medicine.

'This will help you sleep,' she says, shoving the spoon into my mouth. I spit it out.

I don't want to sleep. I'm scared to sleep.

I want Katie.

LYDIA
Sunday July 1st
11.00 a.m.

I wish I didn't look such a mess. The TV people are coming round in a minute and my face is all bloated from crying. Still, I suppose it won't matter; people expect a distraught mother to look sick with worry, don't they? The police say that an appeal from me might do the trick if Katie has just run off out of spite. That nice policewoman is here already; she's just gone upstairs to the loo and to have one more look at Katie's room, although heaven alone knows what she's expecting to find.

'You never know, Lydia,' she told me 'Perhaps Katie's kept letters or a diary – or maybe we'll find out what books she was reading.'

I thought she was going bonkers. What had books got to do with anything?

'Sometimes young girls read something that fires their imagination and they go off to try to relive the fiction,' she said. Sounds a bit bizarre to me, but the inspector said she's not long out of police college and I suppose she's got a lot of fancy ideas.

Mind you, it's given me a chance to clear up the sitting room after the mess that Tom made earlier. I could have done with it being a weekday, and Tom being at Lime Lodge, what with the camera crew coming and everything, but then again, it might add a bit of pathos on the television, me valiantly coping with him in the face of everything that's happened.

He's been a real handful this morning; in fact it's been a long while since he's had such a bad spell. From the moment he got up, he refused to look at me which is always a bad sign. Years ago, he used to be like that all the time, but lately there have been days when he's been quite good at trying to make some sort of contact. Not today, though. Today I might as well be invisible.

All he does is sit in the corner with his back to me and draws pictures of Katie. I know it's Katie because like I said, art is his thing and he gets quite a good likeness when he tries. What upsets me most is that every time he draws her, and I tell him what a good boy he is, he grabs a black felt tip and scrubs her all out. It sends shivers down my spine; I know it's only his way of saying he is angry with her for going off, but it's not comfortable.

There. That's better. The cushions back in place and the toys tidied away. I don't want these TV people to get the idea that we live in a mess. I want them to think I'm a good mother.

That's what I always meant to be. Ever since I was a tiny kid, I dreamed of what it would be like when I had children. I vowed I wouldn't go and die like my mum, or hit my kids like my dad. Only it all went wrong.

I never meant to get pregnant again, not with things the way they were with Him. I'd already made one mistake and I had no intention of making things worse than they were already. When I found out, I was determined to get rid of it – only I couldn't. Three times I went to that clinic, and three times, as soon as I reached the door, I turned round and went home again. I was lucky, I suppose; I wasn't sick or anything so no one guessed. I used to lie awake at night trying to work out what to do.

The letter was like an answer from God – or so I thought at the time. I remember picking it up, recognising the handwriting, and then having to stuff it into my dressing-gown pocket because He was thundering down the stairs, shouting the odds and calling me all names under the sun because breakfast wasn't ready. Funny, really, looking back – that was the morning he hit me so hard that I saw stars. No, really – you read about it in books and think it's just a saying, but I really did see them. Even so, if he hadn't punched me in the stomach, I would probably have just gone on, telling myself he didn't mean it, convincing myself that once he'd got a new job he'd calm down, reminding myself of all his so-called good points. But the moment his fist rammed into my tummy – into my unborn child – I knew.

Of course, I couldn't go there and then. He'd stormed out of the door and I was left to sort things out at home. But I kept re-reading the letter, telling me how loved I was and describing the sort of life I could have – and two days later I went. Leaving Him didn't touch me – but leaving . . .

No. I won't let myself think about it. No point now – and besides, that was the price I had to pay in order to start a new life. I promised myself that the past would stay where it belonged; that I would never tell my new baby the truth and I never have. Until now. Until last weekend when I had that really bad turn and blurted out all that stuff about her father.

And now God has got His retribution and Katie's gone.

There's a van pulling up outside. That will be the TV people, no doubt. I do hope I don't cry. You feel such a fool in front of strangers.

Mind you, I've had a lot of strangers calling today. I've lived here for nearly eighteen months now but I've never got to know the neighbours that well. Now all of a sudden they're turning up with flowers and cakes – that Mrs Driscoll down at number 34 even brought a chicken casserole along, saying that me and Tom had to keep our strength up.

Oh God, there's the doorbell.

'I'll get it!' Brenda, the policewoman, runs down the stairs two at a time. We're on first name terms now – she's really kind and keeps telling me what a good job I'm doing with

Tom. It's not often people appreciate what you go through with a handicapped child.

'Mrs Fordyce! I'm Philip Aubrey, BBC Look East! I am so sorry that we meet in these sad circumstances.'

I shake his hand. He's a nice-looking man, broad shouldered with a mop of fuzzy hair; a bit like an overgrown teddy bear.

'She's being very brave,' Brenda comments as another guy appears with a camera and one of those fuzzy microphone things.

'I've had to be,' I tell them. 'I've not had an easy life.'

I can tell they are all impressed.

People usually are.

KATIE
Sunday July 1st
12.30 p.m.

I'm so scared, I can hardly breathe. How did this happen? How did I get myself into this? I thought Joe loved me, I thought he wanted to take care of me. I even thought, when he came back this morning, that everything would be all right, that he had just overreacted and got paranoid about people finding us.

Now I know it's much worse than that. I don't understand what's happening to him, but it frightens me so much. I have to get away – fast. But how can I, when he has tied my hands behind my back and my right foot to the leg of the table?

Why have I been such a fool? What am I going to do?

Joe left me alone all night. How could he say he loved me and then do something like that?

All yesterday evening, I shouted and kicked against the door of the cottage; I even tried banging the end of the table against it in the hope that it would break down but it was useless; Joe must have nailed it tight shut. When it got dark, I was so scared; I could hear scrabbling sounds in the roof and I was pretty sure it was rats. I wished I hadn't put the sleeping bags in the jeep – all I had were two pillows and the clothes in my holdall.

I suppose I did nod off eventually because I dreamed that Dad was doing woodwork in the garage and I was handing him nails and screws. Suddenly a giant moth flew into the garage, its wings whirring like a helicopter rotor blade. I jolted awake and screamed.

It was Joe; the noise was the cordless screwdriver undoing the barricades on the door.

'Thank God you're back!' I cried as Joe walked through the door and dumped a cardboard box on the table. He grinned, came over to me and enveloped me in a huge hug. The door swung back and forth in the breeze and I realised it was almost daylight.

'Oh, Joe!' I breathed. 'Where have you been? Why did you leave me? What's going on?'

He didn't seem to notice the tears streaming down my face.

'The police are looking for us,' he gabbled. 'It's been on the radio, and I saw your picture on TV in the window of Radio Rentals and ... '

'So let's go home!' I interjected eagerly. 'I mean, Mum will be frantic and ... '

'Good!' he cried. 'Good, good, good!'

There was something in the way he was talking that made me wonder whether he had been drinking – he seemed so hyper and psyched up.

'She's learned her lesson and ... ' I went on, but Joe was having none of it.

'She hasn't even started!' he shouted. 'By the time I'm through Mummy is going to wish she had never been born!'

I tried changing the subject.

'So can we go to the farm? Please?' I asked as calmly as my shaking voice would allow. I thought that once we were in the jeep and on the move I could maybe jump and make a run for it.

Joe moved towards me, smiling broadly, and for a moment I thought he was going to agree. I moved against him and buried my face in his jacket. In the past, he's always been extra gentle when I've been upset. 'I just want to get out of here – I've been so scared and ... '

'Not half as scared as you're going to be!' he laughed, his hands sliding down my back and gripping both wrists. 'This is only the start!'

134

Before I had time to realise what was going on, he had pushed me against the wall, pulled a length of cord from the cardboard box and tied my wrists together.

'Joe! No!' I threw myself against him with all the force I could muster, but he just laughed again and dodged out of the way, so that I fell face forwards onto the floor.

'Joe, if this is your idea of a game, it's not funny!' I was still trying to stay calm, even though my heart was pounding and I could feel the nausea rising in my throat.

'Oh, this is no game, Katie, believe me!'

He threw another length of cord round my ankle and tied it to the table.

I've never felt so vulnerable in all my life – right then, I would have put up with a hundred of Mum's slaps and snide remarks just to get away from Joe.

Then I saw it. Sticking out of the back pocket of his jeans – Joe's mobile phone. I thought fast. If I could grab it and call for help...

I knew it wouldn't be easy. I had to stay calm, lull Joe into thinking I was putty in his hands. I had to let him think it was safe to untie me. And then maybe, just maybe...

'OK, you're right!' I told him breathing as deeply as I could in an attempt to stop the shakes. 'We shouldn't go back – but there's no harm in heading for the farm now, is there? After all, there's no one about and once we are there we can chill out and think things over and...'

'Oh I've been thinking, don't you worry!' he retorted. 'Thinking about Mummy and the wicked things she did, thinking about how she's going to suffer when you don't go home, thinking about how my dad always wanted my mum to know what it felt like to be abandoned. Well, now he's got his wish. That cow of a mother will never get over this.'

'What are you on about?' My attempts at remaining

unruffled were rapidly failing. 'What's your mother got to do with mine?'

For a moment, Joe said nothing. He turned and stared out of the open cottage door, his back to me. The mobile phone was frustratingly close but with my hands tied behind my back I had no chance of getting it.

Suddenly he swung back to face me.

'You just don't get it, do you?' he sneered.

'Get what? What your mother has to do with mine? No, I don't!'

He squatted down beside me, his face only centimetres from mine. There was something odd about him, something I couldn't quite put my finger on.

'They are one and the same, you stupid kid! Your mother is my mother too. The BITCH!'

As he screamed the last word, he slammed his fist into the wall.

'I'm your brother, Katie. The one she left behind.'

I stared at him. He was insane. I don't have a brother apart from Tom. Dad and Mum had to get married in a hurry because I was on the way. Dad told me – not that I'm supposed to let on to Mum that I know. She'd be embarrassed, he said.

'You're mad,' I whispered. 'You can't be my brother...'

'Oh, yes I can!' he snapped. 'My mother walked out on my dad. With you inside her. My dad is your dad – the guy you keep going on about wasn't your real father!'

I caught my breath; I felt as if my throat was closing up.

'My dad is sick now, and hard up and your mother has money and health. And you...'

He kicked my leg so hard that I cried out.

'...you have had everything I should have had! Bitch!'

I felt the glob of spittle hit my face.

'But now,' he went on, 'you're not going to have anything

any more. And what's more, she will find out what it's like to be the one left behind!'

'It's not true!' I heard my own voice shouting back at him, but I felt as if I was sitting way up on the old beams in the ceiling staring down at myself. I saw myself sitting on the floor of my bedroom, looking at those photograph albums; heard myself ask the question.

'*Do I look like my dad, do you think?*'

And, clear as if she was in the room with me then, heard my mother's reply.

'*Why would you want to look like him?*'

It was like an action replay, all the words of that conversation spinning round and round in my head.

'*He never loved you, that's for sure. Not your dad – oh no! He never loved anyone. He didn't know how!*'

And then, the worst part of all.

'*I'll tell you one thing; you've certainly turned out like your father. A vicious, nasty, overweight, overbearing . . .*'

'NO!'

I was crying out at the slowly dawning horror, the unbearable possibility that Joe just might be telling the truth. But Joe thought I was denying what he said.

'Yes!' he yelled. 'Your mum walked out on me. Left a five-year-old kid without a backward glance.'

'You're lying! She wouldn't do that! You're making it up!'

I think I was trying to convince myself as much as him.

Joe gave a short laugh.

'Making it up, am I?' He walked over to the table and rummaged in the cardboard box. 'Well, they say the camera can't lie, don't they? So take a look at that!'

He thrust a photograph into my hand.

'That's what I went back to fetch – that's what you have to see. Look!'

I looked. What I saw staring up at me made me gasp out

loud. It was my mum – younger, slimmer, but unmistakably my mother. And standing at her side, clutching her skirt, was a small, fair-haired boy dressed in baggy shorts and a Mister Messy tee-shirt.

'Is that . . . ?' I couldn't articulate the word. I knew but I didn't want to know.

'Yes, that's me. And that . . .'

He stabbed at the photograph.

'That is my mother! The mother who a few months later walked out and left me. Can you imagine how that made me feel?'

He cupped my chin in his hand and glared at me. And that was when I realised what it was that was different about him. It was his eyes. They were both the same colour.

I blinked and looked again. How could that be? How could his eyes have turned brown overnight?

'Your eyes . . .' I began, but had no chance to finish, because Joe thrust me back against the wall, yanked the rope tighter round my wrists and stood up.

'She's a bitch and now she's going to suffer!'

He snatched the photograph from my hand, stuffed it back into his pocket and wiped the back of his hand across his mouth.

'Do you know what I'm going to do now?' he asked, looming over me.

I shook my head.

'I'm going to see dear Mummy!' He spat the word out. 'I'm going to call on her and watch her suffer! What do you think of that idea – *sister* dear?'

His words made me feel physically sick. I didn't want to be his sister, I wanted – had wanted – to be his girlfriend. My mind was in a whirl – if what he said was true, then my father was a man I'd never seen.

And that was where my strange coloured eyes came from.

'I wonder how our mother's going to feel when I turn up on her doorstep!'

Joe's sneering words snapped me back into the present and my brain went into overdrive. If he really meant it, if he was going back to Hartfield and going to the house, then maybe somehow I could get a message to Mum.

'But surely the police...?' I began, desperate to keep him standing there while I tried to think of some kind of plan.

'I hope the police will be there when I make my visit,' he said eagerly. 'There I shall be, the guy who helped you out at the local Co-op, a travelling sales rep who just happened to hear about your disappearance on the car radio and called to offer his condolences. And if I'm there, I can't be with you, can I? Can't possibly have anything to do with your disappearance.'

He grinned at me.

'By the time they do suss it all out – if they do – it will be too late!'

The words cut into me like ice.

'Wait!'

But it was too late. He had walked through the door, pulled it shut and began screwing the barricade back.

'No, Joe, don't go!' I yelled. 'Don't leave me here!'

'Shit!' The whirring of the screwdriver stopped. In the distance I could hear the low rumbling of an engine.

Then the Land Rover started up and within seconds, I knew Joe was gone.

The engine sound got nearer – I guess it was a tractor. I yelled and shouted and kicked my heels on the floor but of course, no one heard. The cottage is a good fifty metres from the track, tractor engines drown out every sound – and besides, who would expect to find a teenager tied to a table in the middle of nowhere?

I think that this time he's really left me to die.

The police will never find me.

I don't care what Mum did – I don't care what she does to me. I just want her.

I want my mum so much.

LYDIA
Sunday July 1st
6.30 p.m.

I need a drink. I've been very good; I've only had the occasional brandy and the odd little sherry now and again since Katie went missing, but heaven knows, after what happened this afternoon, I need something with a bit of a kick to it. I've had a nasty shock.

Just thinking about it all gives me the shakes. I've been trying to tell myself that it's my imagination, but it's not. It happened. Not that it means anything, of course; it's just one of those awful coincidences – like the day they told us Tom was autistic and every magazine and TV programme for weeks afterwards seemed to be about learning difficulties and special needs.

I'd just sat down with a cup of tea, about five o'clock, I think it was – and I was flicking through one of the old photograph albums that I'd had out for the TV people, when the doorbell rang. It was too early for Grace to be back with Tom – she'd only just left to take him to the swings – and I know it's silly, but for a moment I thought it might be Katie; I jumped up, ran to the door and flung it open.

'Oh!' I'd spoken before I realised it and looking back, I'm not sure whether I cried out in disappointment because it wasn't Katie or in shock because of the familiar face staring back at me. The guy looked just like Him – same floppy hair, same high cheekbones and angular features.

'Hi, I'm Joseph!'

Well, that got me, I can tell you. I felt my legs going weak under me and I remember clinging to the door frame as if my life depended on it.

'Remember me?'

I was speechless. For one awful, heart-stopping moment I thought my past had caught up with me.

He grinned at me.

'I brought the brandy to you with Katie that morning, remember?'

He leaned towards me eagerly, his face alight. That was when I relaxed. It was the eyes, you see; they were brown – ordinary, normal brown eyes like a million other guys across the country would have. I remembered him then; a bit of a poser with sunglasses and attitude.

'Yes, I remember,' I said, wanting to get back to my cup of tea, 'you are the brother of one of Katie's mates, right?'

'I'm rather more than that,' he smiled, 'but if that's what Katie told you...'

Little minx! Still, I'm too worried about her right now to care whether or not she had a bit of a crush on a schoolfriend's older brother.

'I'm afraid Katie isn't here...'

'That's why I've come!' he interrupted. 'I heard the news bulletin and felt I had to drop by to offer you my sympathy.'

He moved really close to me and touched my arm. I caught a whiff of his aftershave – it was one of those smells that you know you know from somewhere but can't quite remember where.

'You must be frantic with worry?'

'I am,' I nodded. 'I can't eat, can't sleep...'

'That's good!' he replied. Odd, I thought, but I suppose he meant that a lot of mothers wouldn't care two hoots about their children's safety.

'But I have to keep strong,' I went on. 'She'll be back, I know she will and...'

'What if she's not?' he interjected. 'What if she never comes back? How will you feel then?'

I went right off him then, I can tell you.

'She will come back,' I said, trying desperately not to cry. 'The police are looking and...'

I stopped because just then, Grace arrived at the gate with Tom. I didn't want her to see me in a state. She doesn't miss much, that one.

'You'll have to excuse me,' I said to Joseph, 'my son is back.'

Most people would have taken the hint and disappeared but this Joseph just stood there, although in the light of what happened next, I bet he wishes he hadn't.

'Run to Mum, then!' Grace said to Tom as she opened the gate. Now Tom has a system with everything. Usually, he comes up the path, stops by the rosebush and sniffs each rose (very irritating that, when it's raining cats and dogs), walks round the broken paving stone twice, and through the front door. But not today.

He stopped dead in his tracks, looked at Joseph and began screaming. And then he did something extraordinary. He didn't back off, as I would have expected with strangers around; he rushed past us both, into the house, up the stairs, and began slamming doors, running from room to room.

'I'll have to go...' I began, but before I could finish my sentence, Tom was back. That's when he threw himself on the ground beside Joe and began hitting him with his fists over and over.

And then he bit him.

Joseph was good about it, I'll give him that. He flinched a bit and swore under his breath and I apologised and tried to drag Tom away. By then he was really in one of his manic moods, throwing himself from side to side, screaming, grunting – totally disconnected from all my efforts to calm him down.

'Just go!' I called to Grace. 'I can manage.'

I could see her eyeing Joseph up and down and just wanted

to be rid of her. It's not that I'm not grateful for all she does, but sometimes you can cope better when you're not being watched.

'I'll pop back later!' she called.

I bet she will too.

'I'll let you get on,' Joseph interrupted – and that's when I got the shock of my life. I'll have to top my glass up because just remembering is bringing the shakes back.

'Mustn't hold you up,' he added, and while he was speaking he was fiddling with his eyes. I thought he'd got a bit of grit in them, or something – or maybe that the pain of Tom's bite had made his eyes water. Men are very sensitive that way.

'Goodbye, Katie's mum!'

He took his hands away and I gasped. He was staring at me, wide eyed, and his eyes were no longer brown. One was green and the other was grey. Like His – and the little one's.

He smiled laconically at me and flicked two used contact lenses off the tips of his fingers and into the flowerbed under the sitting-room window.

Tom was still shouting but it sounded as if the noise was coming from a great distance. I felt the room spin and I willed myself to stay calm.

'I must go!' The words came out cracked and distorted. 'Tom needs his tea.'

'Quite right,' Joseph replied. 'You take care of him.'

He paused and moved even closer to me.

'Do you know, some mothers just walk out on their kids and never go home?'

God, did that freak me out! It was him. Or at least, that's what my panic drove me to think at the time. Now I've had time to think it all through, I keep telling myself that it couldn't be him, that coincidences just don't happen like that, but at the time I felt sick and scared. Who wouldn't be? The

144

guy was called Joseph; he had the eyes – he was even the right age. But then I remembered that Katie had told me he was the brother of some friend of hers and that made me feel a bit more relaxed.

'I must get going too,' he said. 'I've a long journey ahead of me.'

He turned, walked down the path and then paused at the gate.

'I'll come back in a few days,' he said with a smile on his face. 'See how you're coping by then!'

It didn't occur to me until I had shut the front door and cuddled Tom and made some more tea that he was talking as if Katie wouldn't be home, as if he expected to find me in an even worse state when he called again.

It took me ages to calm Tom down. I sang to him, rocked him, even gave him one of his favourite chocolate spread sandwiches, but he just threw it across the room. There are days when I wonder how much longer I'll be able to cope with him and his moods.

I hope Katie's not keen on that Joseph. What if he really is . . . but that's stupid! Of course he's not. He didn't seem very concerned for a boyfriend. I hope he's not using her.

I'm a fine one to talk about using people. I used Jarvis. I've told people all this time how much I loved him but it wasn't true. Oh, I grew to be very fond of him, of course I did; you don't live with someone and have a child by them without some kind of feeling growing between you. But when I married him, I didn't feel a thing except relief. Relief that my baby would be born with a dad – a dad who was convinced that she was his.

I knew that Jarvis fancied me the very first time we met. I'd gone to a nightclub with a couple of girlfriends; my wretched husband was off on a binge weekend with his mates otherwise I could never have accepted the invitation. He hated me going anywhere without him. I wasn't in the mood to go; my period was ten days late and I was pretty sure why. I only went because I thought it would take my mind off everything.

I'd had a few drinks so when Jarvis came up and asked me to dance, I was on my feet and boogying away in an instant. By the end of the evening, we were quite smoochy; he kissed me and told me I was beautiful and asked whether he could see me again.

I knew that I ought to tell Jarvis about Him and about the little one – but I didn't want to. I wanted to feel loved, admired, wanted; so I said yes. One thing led to another that next time and we slept together. Lucky we did; it made convincing Jarvis that Katie was his so much easier – that, and the fact that she looks just like me, apart from the eyes of course.

I mustn't think about the eyes. Joseph has the eyes, and the name and the looks. It was him. No, it wasn't him. I won't let myself believe that. If I did I'd go mad.

But he said those things about mothers...

I've got to stop all this harking back to the past. It's not doing me any good. I need another drink before the police get here. One more won't do any harm. Just to settle me.

Then I'll get Tom his tea.

Not that he will eat it, the mood he's in.

CHANNEL FOUR NEWS
JULY 1st
7.00 p.m.

'Lydia Fordyce, the mother of missing Northamptonshire teenager, Katie Fordyce, today made an emotional appeal for her return. Police now believe that Katie may have run away from home following an argument with her mother. "Katie may think that I'm angry with her," Mrs Fordyce told reporters, "but all I want is to have her back safe and sound." Police have released a photograph of a pair of silver trainers identical to those worn by Katie on the day she disappeared. Anyone with information should contact Northamptonshire Police on 01604 700767.'

KATIE
Sunday July 1st
7.30 p.m.

I've wet myself. I've been bursting for the loo for hours but I kept hanging on, thinking Joe would be back to untie me. I think I must have fallen asleep – I was getting light-headed and faint and my eyes kept closing. Anyway, I woke up with a jolt to find myself drenched and smelly. My hands are tied and I can't even take my knickers off. I feel so dirty.

I feel so sick.

I am so so scared.

My throat is raw from screaming for help and my eyes ache from crying so much. I don't know whether I've cried more about being tied up here, or about the fact that Dad – the man I thought was my dad – isn't. I've gone over and over it in my head; why didn't anyone tell me? Why did Mum walk out on Joe's dad? I can't think of a stranger as my father; I can't get my head round it.

Joe is my brother. We share some of the same genes – we did genetics in Science, DNA and all that stuff. I used to think it would be cool to have a big brother, instead of always having to be the sensible one, the one in charge. But not like this: this is sick.

I mustn't think about it. There's only one thing to think about right now and that's how to get out of here. When Joe comes back – and I have to believe he'll come, otherwise I'd go mad – I'm going to try to get him to take me outside. That way, I can put my idea into action. There's not much chance it will work but I have to try. Joe hates Mum and that's what I have to play on if I'm going to have any chance of getting away. I've been over and over it in my head and I think I could just manage to do it.

Please God, help me. If you get me out of this, I'll do anything. I promise.

Please help me.

LYDIA
Monday July 2nd
2.00 a.m.

Katie! Katie! Over here, Katie! Come back, I'm here!

What? Who?

Oh. She's not here. I was dreaming. Just for a moment...

Oh, where are you, Katie? Are you safe? Are you frightened?

I didn't mean to mess it all up. Everything I did, I did for you – I would never have had the courage to walk out on Him and the little one if it hadn't been for you. I had to keep you safe from his violent temper – and leaving was the only way. I couldn't take the lad – He worshipped him and besides, the child never took to me. We never bonded.

All night I've been tossing and turning, asking myself why I didn't tell Katie the truth? She's old enough – why did I let it all come out the way it did? Why am I such a useless mother?

Dear God, please let her be all right. I'll never shout at her again; she can do what she likes, if only she comes home safe. She can buy silly trainers, wear disgusting perfume...

Oh my God. That's what it was. The perfume. That was the smell. I knew I recognised it from somewhere. Joseph smelt of that awful tacky perfume that Katie's mate sprayed all over her.

What if...? No, that's ridiculous. But supposing she is still seeing him? Supposing they are together?

I'll have to telephone the police station first thing in the morning, tell them about that boy coming to see me and smelling of...

No.

If I do that, it might all come out. Not, of course, that Joseph is THE Joseph, that's impossible.

Just a coincidence.

Look at yourself, Lydia Fordyce. Look in the mirror. Face facts. Stop avoiding the issue. It is him. You know it's him. You are his mother – you can't go on kidding yourself.

And if Katie *is* with him, and if he has told her... or done anything...

I'll phone the police. I don't care what they find out.

I just want Katie home with me.

TOM
Monday July 2nd
9.30 a.m.

My teacher keeps talking but I'm not looking at her. I don't want to look at anything. I don't want to talk. I'm going to hide my eyes so they can't see me.

'Shall we talk about Katie, Tom?'

Katie. Katie's gone.

'Did Katie tell you nice stories, Tom?'

My teacher tries to take my hands away from my face but she can't, because I'm strong.

'Did Katie say where she was going, Tom?'

To the woods. And the farm with the foxes.

'Shall we do some drawing, Tom? And then, if you draw nicely you could have a chocolate lollipop.'

I can hear her pushing paper towards me across the table, then I hear the clatter of felt tip pens as they fall out of the big box.

But I'm not going to look at her.

'If we knew where Katie had gone, perhaps we could find her and bring her home,' says my teacher.

I want Katie to come home.

I pick up a pen.

I open one eye. You need your eyes open to draw but I'm only going to open one.

'Where did Katie go, Tom?'

To the farm with the Joe man. I start to draw Katie. Joe man walking with her.

And foxes.

I know what foxes look like because of the cartoon on the

television. She said she was at Foxes Farm. Animals live on farms.

I can draw lots of animals. I need more paper.

But I'm not going to open the other eye. I like it this way.

LYDIA
Monday July 2nd
11.00 a.m.

I didn't think things could get any worse but I was wrong. I knew when I made the decision to phone them about Joseph and the perfume and everything, that I would be unleashing a whole new can of worms, but I never thought things would come out quite the way they did.

They say they're doing all they can.

They keep giving me strange looks.

I don't blame them. They probably hate me as much as Katie does.

When Brenda turned up earlier, she had a detective inspector with her, one I hadn't seen before. They were hardly out of the car before Grace arrived; she pretended it was just to bring me cake, but personally I think she wanted to hear what was going on. She can be very nosy at times. She said she'd go, but the police inspector muttered something about a cup of coffee being a good start, and that gave her all the excuse she needed.

Of course, the police wanted to know all about Joseph. I told them he came once before with Katie; I didn't mention the brandy because they were sure to get the wrong idea. Was he her boyfriend, they asked? The very thought made me feel sick, and it was on the tip of my tongue to ask them how they thought I was supposed to know, but then that might have made me sound like an uncaring mother, so I just said that he was the brother of a school friend that Katie had a sort of crush on.

'This could be vital information,' the inspector declared.

'I'll get a search set up straight away. I want you to tell me everything – absolutely everything – you remember about this lad.'

'Oh he was tallish, fair hair, brown eyes ... '

I know. But I couldn't. Not then. I just couldn't.

Then, of course, Brenda asked about the perfume. They do keep asking the same questions over and over again, the police; they did it when Jarvis died and to be honest, you end up wanting to shake them. Anyway, I told her yet again that Katie's mate had been fooling about and squirted her with it, but then Brenda suggested that maybe Katie was lying – maybe it was her own perfume and she had squandered her allowance on it and was scared to tell me.

'So let's take a look in her bedroom,' Brenda urged. 'If the bottle is still there, it might help.'

I didn't want to – to be honest, I haven't been in there more than a couple of times since she disappeared. I can't bear to see the unruffled bed and everything so tidy. Still, I followed Brenda upstairs and rifled through Katie's drawer. I found the Anais Anais I gave her last Christmas – I think that's quite suitable for a young girl really – but nothing else.

I was all for getting out of the room, but Brenda flung open the wardrobe door and asked me to sniff. I felt a fool, but suddenly there it was, hitting the back of my throat. I grabbed Katie's angora sweater and sniffed again. It was definitely the same smell.

'We'll take this, if you don't mind!' said Brenda briskly. 'It might just help, you never know.'

I started to cry then – it was just the sight of Katie's clothes and smelling her smell and knowing that she might never come home again.

Brenda plied me with tissues.

'What about money?' she asked. 'Would Katie have had any cash on her?'

'She's got a building society account,' I told her. 'The book should be in her dressing table drawer.'

She went to the dressing table and rummaged about a bit. 'Here!'

She flicked through the pages and then paused.

'Lydia,' she said gently, 'Katie withdrew £150 last Tuesday. I think that just about nails it, don't you?'

She sat down beside me on the bed.

'Katie meant to run away,' she said. 'What we have to do now is find out where she ran to.'

I couldn't stop sobbing.

'You will find her, won't you?'

'We will do our best,' she replied. 'The problem is, Katie may not want to be found. And that always makes our job a whole lot more difficult.'

I knew she was right. And I knew it was because of me that Katie might never, ever be found.

At that moment, all I wanted to do was die.

I pulled myself together in the end, and we went downstairs, only to find the detective inspector talking nineteen to the dozen on his mobile phone.

'Good news!' he announced as soon as we went into the room. 'Our men in Sussex have found the car!'

'The car?' To be honest I was in such a state that I had forgotten all about it.

'The one Katie was seen getting into,' he reminded me. 'A farmer remembers seeing it abandoned at the edge of a quarry backing onto his land, but the following day it had gone. But we've got a registration number and our lads are tracing the owner right now.'

My heart leapt.

'And do you think you'll find her? Do you think . . . ?'

'We're doing all we can,' the inspector assured me, sitting himself down in the chair that used to be Jarvis's. 'Now

156

there are just a few more questions we'd like to ... '

He was interrupted by a screeching of brakes. I flew to the window – every sound raises my hopes. But it wasn't Katie.

It was another police car – and sitting in the back was Mrs Ostler, Tom's teacher. And Tom was with her.

My heart sank. Tom has these fits at times and I thought he'd been ill again.

'It's OK, Lydia!' Brenda jumped up and came over to me. 'The inspector asked Mrs Ostler to meet us here. It seems she has something which she thinks might be significant.'

Her tone of voice implied that she doubted it very much.

'Tom's fine!' Mrs Ostler assured me the moment I opened the door. She pushed him towards me but he just turned his head and began rocking backwards and forwards, banging his hands on the wall. Sometimes you really wish he'd hug you like a normal little boy.

Mrs Ostler touched my arm.

'I'm sorry about all this – I phoned the police because ... '

She hesitated and glanced at the inspector who had stood up to shake her hand.

He nodded, as if to say it was all right for her to talk.

'Tom drew these.' She handed me a sheaf of papers.

I couldn't believe it. Every picture was of Katie – Katie in her silver shoes, Katie with some sort of bag, and then one that made me gasp. Katie with Joseph. Now Tom's only seen Joseph a couple of times yet you could tell it was him. The sunglasses, the floppy hair and in one picture, even the bottle in his hand that he bought for me.

'It wasn't until the weekend, when I heard the news bulletin on the television, that I started thinking,' Mrs Ostler gabbled. 'On Friday, Tom was very distressed and that's when he drew this one – see?'

She stabbed a finger at a picture of Katie with a big black bag.

'I didn't think much of it to be honest,' she apologised, glancing at Brenda. 'He often draws Katie or his mum – it wasn't anything out of the ordinary.'

'Of course it wasn't,' murmured the inspector soothingly, presumably to stop Mrs Ostler feeling guilty.

She smiled.

'But then, this morning, he did all these!'

She gestured to me to take a look, and I began flicking through the pile of papers. There was one drawing with loads of animals in it, and Katie right in the middle of them. Joseph was on the edge of that one, surrounded by what looked like a lot of little red foxes. Another had a lot of trees and Katie in the middle sitting on a rug.

'I think,' said the teacher, directing her remarks to the police, 'that Tom is trying to tell us what he knows.'

Brenda went over to Tom and touched his shoulder.

'Tom? Do you . . . '

Tom's shouts drowned out whatever she had been trying to say.

'Don't touch him!'

Mrs Ostler pulled her away as Tom threw himself bodily onto the floor and began kicking his heels.

'Tom hates to be touched,' she explained. 'Just leave him alone, OK?'

'But if he knows something . . . '

'He's not going to tell us, whatever he knows,' replied his teacher, raising her voice above Tom's repeated shouting. 'He can't – he doesn't have those sorts of communication skills. And if you touch him, he'll simply switch off and go back into his closed little world.'

She thrust his picture into Brenda's hands.

'But what he can do is this! See?'

Brenda gazed at the picture.

'Look,' said Mrs Ostler. 'Katie in her silver shoes; they

158

clearly made an impression with him. And Katie with this boy
– he must be someone that Tom knows.'

'Joseph!'

I'm not sure whether Brenda or I said the word first,
because just at that moment the phone rang. I grabbed it – I
still keep praying every time that it will be Katie.

'Is that you, Lydia?'

I gasped. The years fell away. I think I actually cowered at
the sound of his voice, even though it was on the other end of
a phone. Certainly I put out a hand to steady myself and
knocked a vase off the table.

'You thought you had got away with it, didn't you Lydia?'
Even the inflections were unchanged. 'Thought you could
walk out and leave me and Joe and . . . '

'No! Don't . . . I . . . '

Brenda was at my side in an instant. Everyone in the room
stared at me.

'Who is it?' she mouthed.

I couldn't speak. I couldn't move. I couldn't do anything
except stand there and listen.

'And now you can't even look after the kid you decided to
keep, can you?' The tones grew more sneering with every
word. 'Well, she's gone now, Lydia. You gave up one child;
now we've seen to it that you've lost the other one. She's
gone – gone for good – you've lost her now!'

I heard this long, high-pitched wailing scream and realised
it was me.

'Get a trace on that call – NOW!' The inspector's voice
seemed to be echoing down a long tunnel. And then the room
went black.

I came round in the end of course. The first thing I heard
was Tom's incessant moaning, and the sound of his heels
drumming up and down on the edge of the hearth. For an
instant, I couldn't recall what I was doing lying on the floor

with Brenda bending over me and Grace thrusting a glass of water to my lips.

But I remembered soon enough and then I started to shake. My teeth chattered and I felt sick.

'Shock!' announced Brenda. 'Who was it, Lydia? You have to tell us – who made that call?'

'It was him,' I stammered, the bile rising in my throat so violently that I staggered to my feet, sure that I was going to throw up any minute.

'Joseph? It was Joseph?'

The detective's voice broke in urgently.

I shook my head.

'No, not him,' I said. 'My husband. It was my husband.'

Grace patted my hand.

'No, Lyddy love, you're all confused. Jarvis died, remember?'

She turned to the police officers and I could see her mouthing the word 'suicide' at them.

'Jarvis died,' I repeated. 'But my husband – my first husband – is still alive. And he's got Katie – I just know he has!'

With that I had to dash to the loo. I threw up until I thought that my very guts would end up in the toilet bowl. With every heave, I saw Nathan's face; every time I retched I felt his fists raining blows down on my body. And as I staggered to my feet and wiped my mouth on the towel, I heard his words echoing in my head.

'You worthless, stupid, useless cow!'

I can't stay here inside the loo forever. Brenda has already knocked on the door twice, asking if I'm OK, and I know they won't leave until I've told them everything. I can hear them talking about tracing the phone call – something about it having come from a mobile phone and having to get the permission of some Assistant Chief Constable before they can go any further. And when they do go further, they will find out everything. Everything I did.

I have to face it – the secret's out; the secret I have spent the last fifteen years trying to hide. Fifteen years in which I've avoided going anywhere that He might be, fifteen years of lying and pretending and praying that things would be all right.

But God always has the last word, doesn't He?

I have to face the music and I might as well do it now.

And I have to tell them the whole truth about Joseph.

KATIE
Monday July 2nd
11.30 a.m.

He's back. I can hear the Land Rover bumping over the uneven ground and chugging to a halt.

I have to get this right. It has to work.

It's my last hope.

The jeep door slams. He's coming.

Please God let this work.

The screwdriver whirrs, and I can see the door wobble as Joe removes all the screws. Then it bursts open and light floods in.

'Joe, thank goodness you're back! I've been so worried!'

He moves closer to me.

'She's worried too – our mother! It was so good to see her squirm!'

For a moment my plan goes right out of my mind.

'You saw her? Was she OK?'

'OK? No way – she was frantic!' He smiles smugly as if he's achieved something really clever. 'And my guess is that she's even more worried by now! I bet she's sitting there terrified that her sordid little past is catching up with her!'

I feel my throat closing up as tears well into my eyes. I swallow hard. I have to keep calm.

'Was Tom there?'

'Oh yes, he was there!' he replies. 'That kid is a right nutcase, isn't he?'

I want to yell at him and tell him it's not Tom's fault that he's autistic but I bite my tongue.

'The little brat bit me!' Joe sneers. 'If I hadn't been playing the part of the oh-so-concerned visitor, I'd have socked him one, I can tell you! But I just walked away – promising that I'd be back.'

He savours every word and in my mind's eye I can see him swaggering down the path and...

'So,' I say, desperately trying to ask the next question without seeming too interested, 'did Tom like the jeep? He's car mad!'

I know I'm holding my breath but this matters. It matters a lot.

'Do you think I'm crazy?' Joe is laughing but I know now that my last hope has just gone out of the window.

'As if I'd drive up in the Land Rover for all the world to see! I drove as far as Three Bridges and took the train the rest of the way. Thameslink City Flyer to Bedford, then the Inter City to Kettleborough – just one guy among hundreds! Clever, eh?'

So there was no car parked outside for Mum to notice, assuming she was sober enough to notice anything. I can feel the panic rising inside me. I have to make my plan work. If I'm ever going to get away from here, I have to go for it – now.

'Joe, I'm scared,' I begin. 'Someone was here!'

In the gloom, I can just make out his features – and he looks startled. That's good.

'What do you mean?' He comes over and grabs my shoulder. 'Who was here?'

'These two men,' I lie. 'Or at least, I think it was just two – it could have been more. I heard a car pull up and then there were voices and one of the guys said that it looked as if the door of the cottage had been tampered with.'

Joe looks dead scared. So far, so good.

'Why the hell didn't you tell me? Did you make a noise?' He grabs my arm.

I shake my head.

163

'You told me not to,' I remind him, all innocence. 'But I'm worried because . . . '

I pause.

'Because what?'

'I heard them say that they were going to tell the police and get the place checked over!'

I find myself holding my breath while I wait for his reaction.

'Hell!'

He paces up and down, banging his fist on the side of his head. It reminds me of the way Tom is when things go wrong.

'What time did these guys come?' he demands.

What is the right answer? I want him to think they could be back any minute.

'About two hours ago, I guess,' I say.

'Damn!' Joe bangs his fist against his forehead. 'We can't stay here!'

He wheels round and grabs my arm. This is it. He starts fumbling frantically with the ropes, but the knots have pulled tight with all my wriggling and struggling.

'Hang on!'

He props open the cottage door with a stone so that the morning sunlight shines on me. Even though I'm scared and desperate to get away, I find myself squeezing my thighs together in an attempt to hide the wet patch on my jeans.

'Sit still!'

Joe produces a penknife from the pocket of his jeans and in a few swift slashes cuts me free – first my hands and then my legs.

'Get up!'

I've been praying for this moment and yet now it has come, I find my legs won't obey me.

'What are you waiting for? Get up!'

'I'm trying!' I assure him. 'It's just that I've been tied up for so long and . . . '

'Yes, horrid, isn't it?' he agrees, dropping down onto one knee beside me. 'My dad used to tie me to the leg of my bed when he went to work and...'

'That's awful!' For a second I forgot myself. 'Who would do a thing like that?'

'He had no choice.' To my astonishment, Joe is gently massaging the feeling back into my legs. If I didn't know better, I could almost believe that he was the old gentle, loving Joe. It's as if someone has flicked a switch inside his head and turned the clock back. Or rather, it's as if there are two Joes living in his skin, one loving and kind, the other manic and spiteful.

'If my mother – our mother – hadn't walked out, he wouldn't have had to do it.'

Joe pulls me to my feet. I feel as if my knees are about to buckle under me.

'He had to go to work and so he tied me up,' he says. 'For hours, sometimes.'

'Joe, that's awful!'

I can't help feeling sorry for him – my mother at her very worst would never have done something like that.

'Anyway, what do you care? You with the cushy life and the posh school!'

So much for the gentle Joe. I edge closer towards him.

'Oh, but I do care!' I tell him. 'After all, you're my...' The words stick in my throat.

'... my brother and I'm your sister and...!'

'Shut up! Shut up!' Joe pushes me away. 'I don't want to hear it!'

He shoves me again and then moves away and peers out of the cottage door. The penknife is on the table.

It's not what I'm aiming for, but it's a bonus. I edge nearer, terrified Joe will look round but he's pulling his mobile phone from his back pocket and muttering to himself under his breath. I close my hand over the penknife, and in one rapid heart-stopping moment, stuff it into the waistband of my jeans.

'I need the loo, Joe!' I try to sound pleading and desperate. 'I've got to go, honestly.'

'What?'

I hold my breath, fully expecting him to refuse to let me out of his sight but to my surprise, he just waves a hand dismissively.

'Go on then, but be quick!'

I grab my holdall and begin scrabbling in it.

'What are you doing?' Joe demands, immediately on the alert.

'I just need – women's things,' I say meekly, grabbing a pair of knickers and heading for the door.

'Wait!'

Joe grabs my arm.

'You'll have to go behind the Land Rover,' he says. 'That way you're out of sight if anyone comes down the lane.'

As if. I wish.

'OK!' I mustn't ruffle him now; there is too much at stake.

I've got to be quick; I wriggle my jeans down round my ankles and squat down by the jeep. The relief of being able to go is unbelievable and it feels like I'll never stop. I grab onto the front tyre of the Land Rover to help me keep my balance – and the idea hits me, right out of the blue. Could it work? Will he see me? Whatever, it doesn't matter; I've nothing to lose.

I peep out from behind the jeep, zipping up my jeans as I do so. Joe is pacing up and down in the doorway of the cottage, muttering into his mobile phone. I strain to hear what he is saying but can only catch the odd word.

'... going wrong ... police ... get away ... I CAN'T!'

The last two words are almost a shout and instantly Joe's

eyes dart in the direction of the Land Rover to see if I've heard. There's no time to waste in wondering who he is talking to. I dodge back behind the wheel arch and pull the penknife from the waistband of my jeans.

My fingers are so stiff that, for what seems like an eternity, I can't manage to snap the blade open.

'Go to hell!'

Joe's words drift towards me on the breeze. He's stopped talking. Time is running out.

The blade snaps open and I stab it into the front tyre. I don't know how many slashes it will need to make the Land Rover undrivable so I crawl to the back and do the same on that tyre.

'Katie!' Joe peers out of the door and hisses my name.

'Won't be a minute!' I call. 'Can you get the tissues out of my holdall?'

'For goodness' sake!' he snaps, and I hold my breath. To my relief, his head disappears.

I stuff the penknife into my pocket and I run. I run like I have never run before, stumbling across the uneven ground to the track, my eyes darting from right to left in the hope of finding a way through the thick hedgerow into the field beyond before Joe sees me.

'Katie, what the . . . ? Shit!'

I hear his shouts and fear drives me on. I hear the Land Rover's engine stutter into life and then die. My heart pounds in my ears. I force my legs to keep running. Behind me Joe is trying the ignition again. This time the engines bursts into life, the gears grate, and I know the jeep is moving.

I round a slight bend, not daring to look backwards.

And there, walking down a pathway across one of the fields is the figure of a woman. A woman with a large, bouncy, black dog.

And she's coming this way.

'Help me! Help!'

I might as well be whispering for all the effect it has. I am gasping for breath and my chest feels as if a band of steel is being tightened all round.

'Help me!'

The jeep is gaining on me. I hear the flap flap sound of a deflating tyre but I know it's too late. Another minute and he'll have caught me.

The woman has stopped. She's turned round, her hand shielding her eyes. She's admiring the view, for God's sake.

'You stupid bitch!'

Joe's voice is close. The engine cuts out. The door opens.

'Help!'

I try one last time. The dog's ears prick and it looks this way. The woman doesn't move.

Joe's hands grab me, pinning my arms behind my back.

'Get in!'

He kicks me hard, shoves me against the side of the Land Rover and yanks open the passenger door.

'No, no!'

I struggle but I know it's useless. He's three times as strong as I am and he's angry. Very angry.

'Get in!' He lifts me bodily and hurls me onto the passenger seat, slams the door and runs round to the driver's side.

That's when the woman looks up.

'Bloody hell!'

Joe has seen the tyre.

'Shit!' He kicks the wheel and mutters a few more curses under his breath.

In a second I do the only thing I can think of. I kick off one of my trainers, wind down the window and throw it with all the force I can muster out of the window.

The dog sees it and starts running.

I shout as loudly as I can.

Joe is back in the jeep and his hand strikes my face so hard that for a moment I can't see.

'Shut it!'

He starts the engine and the jeep lurches forward. I pray that the tyres will prevent him from going anywhere, but he stamps on the accelerator, rams the gears and turns the jeep round so that we are heading back in the direction we came from.

'You little cow!' Joe's voice is thick with fury. 'You've done it now! Now I'll have to take you to the farm.'

'I thought that was the general idea!' I sob, grabbing the dashboard as the jeep lurches down the track. 'If you'd done that to begin with, I'd never have . . . '

'I wanted to make it last but now you've blown it!' He grips my wrist with his left hand, his fingernails digging into my flesh. 'Now I'm going to have to do it!'

The two slashed tyres are really deflating now; Joe struggles to keep the Land Rover moving in a straight line.

I stare at him.

'Do what?' The words come out as a croak.

'You'll see!' He lets go of my wrist as the jeep weaves dangerously. He wrenches the steering wheel and I dare to cast a quick look over my shoulder. There's no sign of the woman or her dog.

The wheels are grating on the ground; the jeep swerves, Joe curses and we end up in the hedge.

'Out! Now!'

He leans across me and flings open the passenger door. As he does so, I see his mobile phone sticking out of his back pocket. As he leans across me my fingers touch it but it's too late. He's pulled back and is pushing me out of the Land Rover into the ditch.

'Through there!' He shoves me towards the thick brambles that line the track.

There's a tiny gap, hardly wide enough for my arm. The

thorns scratch my arms and face and tear at my jeans. I wish I hadn't thrown my trainer away; it didn't do any good and now my left foot is hurting like crazy as the brambles pierce my sock.

'This way!' Joe grabs my wrist and begins dragging me along the edge of the field keeping as close to the hedge as he can. 'Faster!'

'Where is this farm anyway?' I gasp, praying that it will be near some other houses, or maybe back onto a road. Anything to give me the chance to get away.

'It's there!'

He doesn't stop running; just jerks his head in the direction of a five-barred gate at the opposite end of the field.

The building on the other side is low and white and there are gaping holes in the roof. Even from this distance, I can see that most of the windows are broken; a piece of torn curtain flutters in the breeze from a window under the eaves, and weeds are growing waist high all round the building.

And there is no sign of life at all.

'Where is everyone?' I pant as we reach the gate. The words 'Fox..l. Fa.m' are scratched into the mildewed wood; a rusting bicycle leans against the fence.

'There's no one here – just you...'

Joe leans forward, gripping his side and panting for breath.

'...and me.'

My heart sinks. All my hopes about finding a phone, or getting one of Joe's mates to make him see sense evaporate into thin air.

'You said... what about the other guys? Flip and Ellie and...'

'I lied,' he snaps. 'They don't exist. Don't you see?'

I can feel the scream rising in my throat.

'But why? Why?'

My fists are pummelling his chest; he pushes me away with a sneer.

'Because he wanted our mother to be punished. Because he trusted me to make it happen. He said I had to find a way of getting you to come with me, and I did!'

He beams at me and drags me down the path towards the door of the bungalow.

'He'll be dead proud of me when I've done it!'

And suddenly I get it.

'Your father!' I gasp.

It's not a question, it's a statement. His father wants me hurt so that Mum will suffer.

I feel as if I'm going mad. My eyes dart all round, from left to right. There's nowhere to run. A wind is getting up and clouds are scudding across the sun.

Suddenly, Joe's phone rings.

'Damn!'

He snatches it from his pocket

'Yes. Soon. I'll tell you when, OK?'

I can hear a faint, deep voice on the other end, and start thinking. Fast.

'Just let me deal with it my way, OK!'

Joe punches the End Call button and turns to me.

'I'll stay for a bit,' he says, kicking open the door of the farmhouse. 'I won't go yet.'

He looks at me, as if expecting praise for his kindness.

I force myself to smile.

If I can just keep him sweet, if I can just get hold of his phone, then maybe someone will come and get me.

Please God, let someone come and get me.

GRACE
Monday July 2nd
12 noon

She's going to pieces, not that you can blame her. What a morning! It's like living in the middle of one of those detective thrillers you see on the telly, the kind where you tell yourself it's all a bit far fetched. I wish it was. I wish this was all a story.

She looks like death, like she's seen a ghost, but at least she's upright again. The policewoman was getting really edgy, standing outside the loo door and muttering something about breaking the door down if she didn't come out soon. I think she thought Lydia might do something stupid, but I knew she wouldn't. Not like Jarvis.

Poor man. I mean, I know they say it's a sin to take your own life, but all those debts! Who would have thought it – he seemed such a level-headed, sensible type and I should know, because I've seen them through some sticky moments over the years. When Lydia had her breakdown, he was rock solid behind her. Something inside his head must have flipped to make him do what he did and I reckon it could have something to do with what's going on right now. Mind you, Lyddy talking about another husband could just be down to the drink, you never can tell.

I'm glad I popped over, though. Bill says I am just being nosy, but it's not that at all. I saw a police car heading for Lydia's house and since I'd made some jam tarts and a bit of flapjack, I thought it would be a good time to take some over. So I popped some in a Tupperware box and went across.

That's not being nosy; it's being neighbourly.

172

And the police must have been pleased too, because while Lydia was retching her guts up in the toilet, and the teacher was trying to calm little Tom down, I took them all some coffee. That nice inspector seemed very agitated when I went in, so I lingered a bit to see if I could help.

'We've got the ACC's consent and we've contacted the service provider,' he was telling the young constable. 'They've just told us that the mast that picked up the signal from that last call was situated in Brighton. Narrows things down a bit, doesn't it?'

'That's where Lydia used to live!'

Perhaps I shouldn't have blurted it out like that, but I couldn't help myself.

The inspector looked round, as if surprised to see me there.

'Ah, Mrs Wheeler,' he said. 'Known Lydia a long time then, have you?'

So I told him about the children's home and about catching up with Lyddy on the train that day – I made sure I stressed that it was a train from Brighton – and how I'm Katie's godmother and he jotted it all down in his book.

'You live opposite, don't you?' he said. 'I wonder, did you by any chance see Katie leave for school on Friday?'

I shook my head. I didn't have to think; I've done mental reruns of that day a hundred times since then.

'I usually do,' I told him. 'I walk my dog about eight o'clock, and usually, I see Katie leaving the house, just as I'm on my way back up the road. On Friday there was no sign of her.'

'And when you got home, had the refuse collection van already cleared your rubbish?' he continued, scribbling in his notebook.

I couldn't work out what relevance that had, but I racked my brains and nodded.

'Yes, they had,' I said. 'I know because Whisky – that's my dog – usually sniffs all round the bags and I have to yank her

173

away. On Friday, they had already gone.'

The inspector turned to Tom's teacher who was standing there looking as if she wished she could be any place else.

'It fits,' he said. 'The dustcart came early – we can easily check the exact time. And with these...' He waved Tom's drawings in the air. '...it could be the start of something helpful.'

'Could I see them?' I asked. I couldn't help myself.

The inspector passed the papers to me and the bottom sheet fell to the floor. I stooped to retrieve it and gasped out loud. It was a picture of Katie – Katie in red pyjamas and silver shoes. Beside her was a huge black bin bag, out of all proportion to the rest of the picture.

'Tom did all this?' I asked Mrs Ostler. 'All of them?'

The teacher nodded.

'It's his way of communicating,' she explained, as if I didn't know the first thing about the lad. 'This bag is so huge because that's the bit he sees as important.'

Just then, Brenda, the policewoman, came back into the room, supporting Lydia who looked as if she was about to pass out all over again.

'Lydia's ready to talk now,' she told the inspector and it struck me that some of the old friendliness had gone out of her voice.

'I don't know where to start...' she murmured.

'Let me help,' declared the inspector, standing up and strolling over to the window in that nonchalant way they do on 'Inspector Morse'. 'That phone call from Nathan Tucker came from the Brighton area – we know that because we've located the mast and determined the strength of the signal.'

'So you'll find her...?'

'We've got the Sussex police on the case right now,' he assured her. 'You lived in Brighton in the past – with Nathan.'

It wasn't a question; it was a statement.

174

Lydia nodded imperceptibly and glanced up at the teacher.

'We will talk more about that later,' said the inspector. 'Meanwhile, I'd like you to think back to Friday morning. That's refuse collection day and...'

'Wait!'

Lydia stopped dead in the middle of the room.

'The van – it came while I was...'

She paused.

'I had a tummy bug that morning,' she said, glancing hastily at me. 'I was in the bathroom feeling unwell and trying to cope with Tom who was in a right state. That's when I heard the dustcart...'

Actually, she said 'custdart', on account of her agitation.

'Katie rushed to the door and said she had just remembered that there was another rubbish bag to go out,' Lydia went on. 'I heard the door slam and...'

Her voice faded and she stared at the policewoman.

'And that was that,' she whispered.

'But what would the rubbish have to do with Katie's disappearance?' The teacher was clearly as confused as I was.

Brenda took the paper from me and stared at it once more.

'Katie is wearing red trousers...'

'Pyjamas,' I corrected her.

All three of them stared at me.

'Pyjamas?' Brenda mouthed

'That's right,' Lydia affirmed. 'The ones with Winnie the Pooh on the front. I told her she was getting too old for that kind of thing but...'

She sank into a chair, her head in her hands.

'Wait!' Brenda interrupted. 'Tom obviously saw her dressed like that – and yet you say that both he and Katie were with you that morning when the dustcart came?'

Lydia nodded.

'Katie was up and dressed really early that day,' she went on. 'Said she wanted to get to school to . . .'

Her voice broke.

'I think,' said Brenda, thoughtfully, 'that Katie was hiding something the night before – hiding it outside the gate and that's what Tom saw.'

She turned to his teacher.

'Is that possible?'

The teacher nodded.

'He would have been agitated by anything that deviated from his normal routine,' she agreed. 'Katie out in the street in her night clothes would certainly have stayed in his mind.'

Well, after that there was a lot of note taking and phone calls and I went into the kitchen to make myself useful getting more coffee for everyone. When I went back into the room, I caught the tail end of the conversation.

'Why didn't you tell us that she was seeing this Joseph fellow?' the detective inspector was asking. 'I would have thought that a boyfriend would have been the very first person you contacted.'

'He's not her boyfriend! He can't be!'

The inspector raised one eyebrow, clearly surprised by the vehemence of Lydia's retort. Mind you, she's always been pleased that Katie isn't boy mad, not like some of them you see in the shopping mall on a Saturday, all draped around the guys with skirts up to their armpits.

'What I mean is,' Lydia murmured, 'well . . .'

Brenda touched her arm.

'Lydia, we need to know anyone who might have some idea about Katie's movements – it's very important.'

Lydia nodded and then broke into a smile.

'Oh, all I meant was that these young girls – they have crushes on all sorts, don't they?'

She looked across to me as if pleading for agreement.

'She mentioned that this Joseph was the brother of some kid in her class – but she told me there was nothing in it. Nothing at all. Just mates.'

'That's what they all say,' muttered the inspector.

Brenda whipped out her notebook.

'Do you have a surname?' she asked.

Lydia looked uncomfortable.

'She said the guy was Antonia's brother,' she murmured. 'I can't be expected to remember the surname of every kid in her school.'

'We'll check!' Brenda flipped the notebook shut and stood up. 'Now why don't you try to get . . . '

She stopped in mid-sentence as her radio phone bleeped.

'Yes? That was quick. He does? Brilliant! I'll tell her.'

She looked up with a faint smile on her lips.

'One of the guys who works the dustcarts remembers Katie,' she announced. 'He heard the item on this morning's news – it was his day off – and he rang the station at once.'

'Does he know where she is?' You could see that Lydia realised the answer before she finished asking it.

'No,' Brenda replied gently, 'but he does remember her dashing from the house and grabbing one of the bin bags from him, saying that she never meant to throw it away in the first place.'

She paused to let the impact of her announcement register. I think the other two were just as bewildered as I was.

'What's even more important,' Brenda went on, 'is that he looked back a minute later and saw Katie hurrying off down the road with a blue holdall in her hand!'

Lydia gasped.

'The blue bag?' She jumped up and ran into the hall. Two seconds later she was back.

'It's gone,' she said. 'It's not in the cupboard.'

'Don't you see?' Brenda urged. 'Katie had clearly hidden

something outside the house the night before! Clothes, maybe, cash – who knows?'

She paused again.

'Which makes it almost certain that Katie did intend to go away,' she stressed. 'She may well have had it all planned – which would appear to rule out abduction.'

That's when Lydia broke down and lost it completely. She just sobbed and howled and wailed like an injured animal. I couldn't understand it; I would have thought that she would have taken heart from the fact that Katie was probably with a friend somewhere. Brenda tried to tell her that Katie might have gone to London, that the police would search all the hostels, but it didn't seem to make any difference.

'If I hadn't let it slip...won't come back...I didn't go back...God punishing me.'

None of it made any sense.

'We'll get in touch with all her school friends,' Brenda said, stroking her arm gently. 'Teenagers often tell their mates things they wouldn't dream of admitting at home. Perhaps one of them knows why she never went to the party.'

'They all know that!' Lydia snapped. 'Katie told them on Thursday that I wouldn't let her and...'

She stopped, her hand flying to her mouth.

'What is it?' The inspector stepped forward, and looked intently at Lydia.

'Oh God!' breathed Lyddy. 'Alice – that's my daughter's best friend – she told me on the phone that Katie had moaned to her on Thursday about not being allowed to go to Mandy's sleepover.'

'So?'

'Katie and I never discussed the party until Thursday evening when I got in from her Parents' Evening,' Lyddy went on. 'So if Katie was telling everyone that she couldn't go, but was wanting me to say she could...'

The inspector nodded.

'It all points to the fact that Katie had other plans all along,' he finished. 'We need to find this Joseph lad, and see whether he has any information.'

Lyddy went really pale at that. I guess it's worrying when your daughter gets to the boyfriend age. It's pretty worrying when your son gets to the boyfriend age too.

'I could phone Alice – that's Katie's best friend,' gabbled Lydia hurriedly. 'She'll know – boy mad, that girl is. She'll know it's not Joseph.'

'Not Joseph?' Clearly the police constable was confused.

'I mean – she'll know that this Joseph person isn't going around with Katie,' Lydia blundered on, snatching up the handset and punching in a number. 'I would have known.'

Hardly, I thought to myself, considering half the time you don't know what time of day it is.

'Alice? Katie's mum here. What? No, she's not. Listen, Antonia is in your class, isn't she? Yes, well, does she have a brother? She does!'

She turned and nodded to Brenda.

'What? Daniel? How old? Oh. Right. No, it's just that there's this guy Joseph who Katie seems to have some kind of crush on and... What?'

Her hand flew to her mouth.

'What do you mean, you thought it was all over? Called what? Joe.'

She let the handset fall from her hand and clunk onto the sideboard.

'No,' she whispered. 'Please God, no.'

Brenda was at her side in an instant.

'What is it?' she urged, leading Lydia to a chair.

'Alice says that Katie was seeing a boy called Joe months ago,' Lydia whispered. 'Dead keen, she was, Alice said – but then she stopped talking about him and Alice assumed he had dumped her.'

She put her head in her hands.

'Lydia, don't worry!' Brenda said soothingly. 'This could be a great help. If this Joseph is seeing Katie again, he probably knows where she is. At the very least, he may know how her mind works – she might have been planning this for months.'

'No, just a few days I guess,' Lydia murmured, breaking into sobs. 'Since I said what I did about ... well, since we had our argument.'

'We'll find Joseph,' said the detective, standing up and walking towards the window. 'Whatever he knows, we will know within a few hours, don't you worry!'

'No!'

Lyddy jumped to her feet

'I mean – yes, yes, of course you must,' she said sinking back into the chair.

'Are you sure you can't add anything to the description you gave us? Fair hair, brown eyes ...'

'They were brown to start with.' Lydia's voice was flat and expressionless.

The detective frowned.

'To start with?'

He glanced at Brenda who shrugged imperceptibly.

'He was wearing coloured contact lenses,' replied Lydia, looking over his shoulder at the blank wall. 'I didn't realise that, of course, until just before he left when he took them out and his eyes were ...'

She hesitated and I swear she turned even paler than before.

'Yes?'

The detective's pen was poised over his notepad.

'Odd coloured – one was green, and the other grey.'

180

I gasped.

Brenda's eyes widened.

You could have heard a pin drop.

'Like your daughter's?' Brenda was the first to speak.

Lydia nodded.

'Like hers,' she said, forcing a smile. 'Quite a coincidence, isn't it?'

There was a long silence.

'Only,' she whispered, so faintly that I had to strain to catch what she was saying, 'only I don't think it is a coincidence.'

Her hand flew to her mouth and she bit down on her knuckles.

'You see, I think Joseph is my son. That was his father on the phone. Nathan. Nathan Tucker.'

Well, I was speechless. I couldn't take in any of it. It didn't make sense. But before anyone had had the chance to speak, the inspector's phone bleeped.

'Yes? What? Now we're getting somewhere!'

He thumped his fist against his thigh and looked up at Brenda.

'The car is registered in the name of Nathan Tucker,' he said. 'And what's more the Road Fund Licence hasn't been paid – it's supposed to be off the road!'

'So Nathan's got her! Oh my God!'

Brenda moved swiftly to Lydia's side – she looked as if she was about to pass out all over again.

'Wait!'

The inspector clicked his fingers as if making a snap decision.

'Mrs Fordyce,' he began. Not Lydia, this time, I noticed, and not much sympathy for her delicate state. 'In view of what you have just told us and of these latest developments, I think it would be very helpful all round if you would come to the station with us, just so that we can verify your story.'

'But what if Katie phones? Or comes back?' Lydia began.

'The constable here will remain in the house until you get back,' he announced. The constable looked pretty peeved at the idea.

'Well, I don't know... there's Tom to think about,' Lydia tried again.

'Mrs Fordyce, time could be running out for Katie,' he replied sternly. 'And you haven't exactly been forthcoming with information for us.'

'I'll look after Tom,' Mrs Ostler said. 'We'll go back to school and he can wait with me till this is sorted.'

So Lydia and Brenda went off and that's when I came home. I needed to get my head around everything. None of it makes any sense at all. How can this Joseph be Lydia's son? When the police asked her, she put his age at around nineteen; Katie's fifteen. And Lydia certainly didn't have a child when I went down for the wedding.

Unless...

Dear God, no. Surely not. No.

But all that illness and the nightmares and...

She couldn't.

She wouldn't.

Not even Lydia at her very worst would do a thing like that.

Would she?

KATIE
Monday July 2nd
3.00 p.m.

I thought it was going to be all right. As soon as we got here, I started to talk and talk, and Joe seemed to be listening. I convinced myself that somehow he would see sense and take me home. He was so close to doing things my way, I know he was.

And now it's all gone horribly wrong.

After we arrived at the farm, he seemed strangely ill at ease, as if suddenly he didn't know what to do. The place was a tip, but not as bad as the cottage. It looked as if someone had lived here once – there were old newspapers stacked in one corner, and even a few logs by the crumbling fireplace. Joe lit a few candles and produced a bar of chocolate which we shared. I figured if he really wanted me to die, he wouldn't keep giving me things to eat. All the time my brain was racing, trying to think of a way to escape. I knew the road was a good two miles up the track; it was pointless to try to make another run for it. Even though the Land Rover was useless, Joe was much fitter than me and I hadn't even got two shoes any more.

For a long while, Joe was unusually silent. I kept quiet too, terrified of saying anything that might inflame his temper again and make him do something drastic. He kept looking at his watch and pacing up and down. Then suddenly, his mobile phone rang.

'Yes? Yes, I have. No! Not yet! Because I say so, OK? NOT YET!'

He slammed the phone down on the table.

'Who was that?'

I knew the answer, but I had to do all I could to play for time.

'My dad,' he replied. 'Your dad.'

He stared at me.

'He wants me to – to get going,' he muttered.

My thoughts began racing ahead. If he went, he had two choices; to take me with him or to leave me behind. Either way, my chances of escape would be better than they were now.

'So hadn't you better go?' I began. 'I mean, you said he was sick and ...'

'I'll go when I'm bloody ready, OK?' he shouted. 'He's always telling me what to do, calling the shots ...'

He broke off and leant back against the wall. His face, lit by the light of the flickering candles, looked suddenly much younger, more uncertain. The phone was on the table beside him; I had to keep his attention away from that.

'He's so damn dictatorial!'

Joe thumped his fist against the wall.

'God, I know what you mean!' I burst out. 'Parents! Think they own us half the time!'

Bad move.

'Our mother didn't think that, did she?' He spat out the words and moved towards me. 'She didn't give me a second thought when she walked out on my father!'

'Oh, but she did!'

I don't know what made me say that, but the moment I saw him falter, heard a sharp intake of breath, I knew I had to build on it.

'What? What do you mean?'

There was a kind of desperation in his voice, so unexpected that I almost felt sorry for him.

'Well, you know that day you bought the brandy? The day you came to the house with me?'

I hesitated. I had to make the story sound plausible and I hadn't a clue as to how I was going to do it.

'What about it?'

'After you'd gone,' I went on, 'Mum said that she thought you were really nice. And then she went all quiet and sort of sad for ages.'

In truth, she'd quizzed me for ages about who Joe was and then gone and got drunk again, but this was no time to be sticking to the facts.

Joe didn't say anything but at least he was listening.

'She said that once, a long time ago, she'd had a little boy and . . . '

'Yes?'

Joe was leaning forward, watching me intently. That's when I almost lost the plot. I knew I couldn't pretend that she'd admitted to walking out on him; if she had really done that I wouldn't have been so surprised about having a brother. So I said the first thing that came into my head.

Stupid dumb me.

'She told me that he had died,' I murmured.

With that, Joe went ballistic.

'The bitch! She said that? Her own kid and she makes out I'm dead! Well, soon she'll discover what it's really like to have a child die on you!'

I opened my mouth but no sound came out.

'You want to know what really happened?' He didn't wait for an answer. 'Well, I'll tell you. She walked out and she took eight hundred pounds of my dad's money with her! She didn't leave a note, she didn't even kiss me goodbye!'

His face was scarlet and his fists clenched. And he was looking at me as if it was all my fault.

'She didn't even stay to finish the jigsaw puzzle.' His voice now was childish, petulant even.

He began pacing up and down.

'Do you know, I waited every day for her to come back? My birthday came and went and she didn't even send a card! Can you imagine what that was like for a kid of five?'

I couldn't. How could she have done that? Why? If Joe was her son – and I knew he was – why didn't she take him with her? It would be like walking out on Tom. Or me. And whatever Mum did on a bad day, she would never, ever give up on us.

Never.

'Of course,' Joe blurted out, 'my dad didn't know then that she was pregnant – with you!' He spat out the last two words. 'That she'd stolen his kid as well as his money!'

'But she wasn't...'

My mind was racing.

'She got pregnant the very moment she married my father...'

'Your father is my father!'

I tried to keep my temper.

'Joe, honestly, listen to me – Mum got pregnant with me the very night of their honeymoon – her and Jarvis's, that is.'

Joe stared at me. Then he threw back his head and laughed.

'You poor pathetic kid!' he shouted. 'You don't really believe that, do you? She conned that Jarvis bloke into thinking you were his. She'd been having a fling with him, the two-faced slag!'

'How do you know all this?' I yelled back. 'You've already told me that your dad didn't know she was pregnant, so how come you're so knowledgable, all of a sudden?'

'Because,' he threw back, 'my dad's no fool! After she left, he asked around, chatted to her workmates, found out that she'd been seeing this guy called Jarvis.'

'There you are then!' I felt triumphant. 'I mean, OK, she was wrong to have an affair, but it proves that Jarvis is my dad!'

'You reckon?' Joe retorted sarcastically. 'Well, you're wrong! Because a few months later, my dad was on a bus and he spotted her in the street, with this huge belly!'

I knew he hadn't finished.

'She was with a guy and he was laden with bags from that shop – what's it called? Mothercare!'

'But that doesn't prove...' I began.

'My dad got off the bus at the next stop and tried to find her but he couldn't – not then,' Joe said. 'But a year later, he was doing a building job in Brighton and he saw the guy pushing a baby in a buggy.'

His voice dropped.

'It was this Jarvis bloke. My dad went up to him, to have it out, find out where my mother had gone. And that's when he realised.'

I was about to say, 'Realised what?' but I didn't bother. I already knew what Joe was going to say.

'He looked at the baby in the buggy,' he went on, 'and the baby looked straight back up at him. Its eyes – your eyes – were just like his and just like mine.'

Joe ran his fingers through his hair and rubbed his temples.

'And you know what?'

His voice cracked and he turned away.

'What?' I took a step closer to the table, a step closer to the mobile phone.

'That's when Jarvis offered to buy you off my dad!'

My hand was already reaching for the phone as Joe wheeled round to face me. I dropped it to my side and pretended to be scratching my thigh.

'That's ridiculous!' I exploded as soon as the full impact of his words hit me. 'He wouldn't...'

'He did! My dad told him to have a blood test if he wanted proof that you were his and that's when Jarvis said he'd pay my dad money every month, just as long as he would keep his

187

mouth shut and never go near you or him ever again. So my dad agreed.'

I felt sick. How could he do that? How could either of them do those things? It was bad enough that my dad – I mean, Jarvis – would buy someone else's baby, just like that; but even worse that Joe's father – my father – would take cash for me, like I was some secondhand car.

'*He knew nothing about love, that's for sure!*'

Mum's words echoed in my head. I remembered not just what she said, but the way she said it, as though she was hurting badly inside. It was true that she had been drunk at the time, but the thought suddenly struck that maybe, after all, it hadn't been my dad she was talking about – Jarvis, that is. Could it be that she was thinking of Joe's father?

'Dad watched you, though, both of you!' Joe shouted. 'He's not stupid, my dad. Every time you moved house, that Jarvis would be late with a payment – I guess he thought he'd shaken us off. But Dad always caught up with him and each time, he made him pay for trying to cheat on him.'

I swallowed hard.

'What about Mum?'

I had to know. I had to know how big a part she had in all this sordid, horrible mess.

'Her? She didn't know a thing!' Joe blurted out. 'Every time Dad threatened to confront her, Jarvis upped the odds, paid him more money. Said he loved you all so much that he couldn't bear to have you hurt. Silly sod!'

My eyes filled with tears. So he did love me! I was right – Dad loved me. Never mind that he wasn't my biological father; he was the only one I knew. All that matters is that he had cared.

'So why does your dad want to hurt me?' I stammered. 'Surely, if I'm his own daughter...'

As I spoke, an idea formed in my mind.

'...he'd like to meet me, get to know me?'

Joe opened his mouth but I couldn't afford for him to change the subject.

'Why don't you take me to him? I'd love to meet him – I mean, he is my father, after all!'

Joe frowned.

'That's not the plan...' he began. 'He never said I was to do that.'

He turned and began pacing again. I took a step nearer the mobile phone, praying and talking at the same time.

'Or maybe instead, you could come and see my mum, and tell her who you really are and...'

Once again, I had said the wrong thing.

'Oh sure!' Joe sneered. 'And get myself nicked for taking you away with me? Hardly!'

'You'll get nicked if you don't take me back!' I retorted. 'You said yourself that the police are looking for me. But if you take me home of your own free will, and I say that you are my long lost brother and pretend that going off was all my idea, well that would be OK, wouldn't it?'

I knew I was gabbling but at least he was listening.

'My mum will be frantic by now! You've made her pay for what she did. Surely your dad will be satisfied with that?'

Joe gave a short laugh.

'Satisfied? He might have been if that Jarvis hadn't gone and died when he did. Just as Dad was about to play his trump card.'

'What?' I was getting confused all over again.

'Our nasty little mother married the precious Jarvis, didn't she?' Joe demanded.

'Of course she did,' I agreed, trying to ignore the malice in his voice. 'They had to – she was expecting...well, you know that.'

'What she didn't do,' mocked Joe, 'was divorce my father first.'

189

'You mean ... ?'

I was certain I'd got it wrong.

Joe nodded.

'Bigamy,' he said. 'She was married to two men at the same time. Dad only found out by accident – he'd assumed they were just living together. Jarvis never wore a ring or anything.'

I shook my head.

'He didn't even wear a watch,' I told him. 'He had this skin condition, an allergy to metal and ...'

'Anyway,' interrupted Joe, 'it was Jarvis who let it out of the bag. He'd missed a payment and my dad threatened to turn up on the doorstep and Jarvis said he mustn't because it was their wedding anniversary and he'd meet him a few days later with the cash, plus a bit for staying away.'

He kicked the wall.

'That's when Dad decided to go for it big time. He told him he had two weeks to get £10,000 to him or else he'd go to the police and tell them that your mum was married to two men.'

I gasped.

'£10,000? That's ridiculous!'

I knew Dad didn't have that kind of money.

Joe shrugged.

'I said it was too much,' he nodded. 'But Dad was out of work and I guess he thought he'd try his luck. Only Jarvis went and died, didn't he? That very night!'

That's when I lost it.

'And your dad killed him! That's what he meant in the note – he couldn't find that kind of money! So he locked himself in the garage and took the hose from the vacuum cleaner and ...'

I sank down on the floor. I couldn't stop crying. I could see it all again; see myself going to the garage to get my bike and

190

finding it locked. Fetching the key and then throwing open the door. I could smell the stench of the carbon monoxide making me gag, see Dad, grey and still, slumped over the steering wheel. I could hear myself screaming, screaming, screaming; hear Mum's footsteps running from the house, see her fists beating up and down, up and down on the roof of the car and . . .

'Don't cry!'

Joe's hand was on my shoulder. It took every ounce of self control in me not to push him away but if he was softening, I had to play on it. And I had to think fast.

'So why didn't your dad go and see my mum? Ask her to help out?'

The question seemed to take Joe by surprise.

'I don't know,' he admitted. 'I guess there was no point – I mean, it was the money he was after and the TV news people said that Jarvis was deeply in debt, didn't they? Made a big thing of it and . . . '

'You don't have to remind me!' I snapped back. 'And now we know why, don't we? Mum could never understand it – Dad had always been so careful with money, tight even. We never had expensive holidays, or flash cars; it wasn't until we found . . . '

I stopped. There was no need for Joe to know about the pile of crumpled betting slips that the police found in Dad's pocket – Dad who had never gambled in his life, who wouldn't even buy a Lottery ticket because he said it was as dumb as burning banknotes on your front lawn.

It all fell into place. He'd obviously started betting on horses in the hope of winning enough to pay off Joe's dad.

'But at least you had a mother!'

Joe wasn't shouting; his shoulders sagged and he slumped down to the floor and put his head on his knees.

'I didn't and now I don't know what to do!'

191

He was crying. For a moment, I had the urge to go across and comfort him, but I knew that if I missed this opportunity, it might never come again.

I reached out, grabbed the mobile phone, stuffed it into the back pocket of my jeans and then leaned against the wall, praying that he wouldn't notice.

I've been leaning here now for at least five minutes and Joe hasn't moved. I daren't go to the door because that will alert him to my plan. I can't risk making a call; the keypad bleeps every time you strike a number and he'd be on me in seconds.

'Joe, what's that? OH, God, Joe – look!'

He's on his feet in an instant, darting to the door.

'What? What is it?'

'I saw someone,' I cry. 'They went round the back.'

He steps outside, his hand still on the doorpost.

I have to risk it.

I have to do it now.

I snatch the phone from my pocket. My hands are trembling so much I can hardly punch in the numbers.

'9-9-9!'

Joe is still looking out of the door.

'Which service, police, ambul...'

'Police!'

I hiss, not daring to raise my voice above a whisper.

Joe is turning back.

'Police – can I help...?'

'Help me, please. He's going to hurt me. I'm at Foxhole...'

'YOU LITTLE BITCH!'

Joe is on me. He snatches the phone, hurls it to the ground, and hits me round the face.

I scream.

'HELP ME!'

As I try to run, he grabs my arm, throws me to the floor, kicks me, once, twice, three times.

I can hear my shouts as his fist beats into my head.

'He was right! Women are all evil, two-timing, twisted cows! Well, you've had it now!'

He kicks me again, this time in the ribs. The pain is like a searing hot blade cutting through my body.

'I didn't want to do this, OK!' Joe is sobbing and shouting at the same time. 'You know what I really wanted? I wanted you to love me!'

He is down on his knees beside me now, his face only centimetres from mine, his stale breath hot against my cheek.

I force myself to lift my head a fraction. Joe's face is wet with tears and he rubs at his eyes like a small boy.

'I kept thinking how I could punish you without killing you,' he shouts. 'But now you've done it – now I have to do what he says!'

He scrambles to his feet, scrabbles wildly in his pockets and pulls out a box of matches.

He's striking one and holding the flame up against my face.

'Joe! No! Don't!'

'I have to,' he says. 'My dad wants it this way.'

'But it's not fair on you!' My mind is racing. I force myself to quell the rising wave of nausea and concentrate on buying time. 'Why should you do all the dirty work for your dad? If he wants to kill me, let him do it himself!'

Joe says nothing. He just stares at me.

'I mean, think about it, Joe,' I stammer, in between searing stabs of pain. 'You do this – you'll get caught and go to jail, and he gets off scot-free. I mean, he's not going to . . . aaah!'

The pain when I move is like nothing I've ever known before.

'Not going to what?' Joe seems oblivious to my agony

193

but at least he's let the match burn out and he isn't lighting another one.

'He's not likely to admit that it was all his idea, is he? But of course, if you were to tell the police the whole truth, they'd realise it wasn't your fault and...'

'The police aren't going to know!' Joe yells, striking another match. 'Because by the time they get here – if they get here – you'll just be a lump of charred flesh!'

Now I know. He's insane. And I'm going to die.

LYDIA
Monday July 2nd
4.45 p.m.

I need a drink. Not, of course, that they're about to give me one here, only endless cups of tea to accompany their endless questions. I'm not under arrest or anything. They make a great point of saying that over and over again – it's just that they feel I should be on the spot at the incident room because things are moving so fast.

I've told them the whole story – about Nathan beating me to a pulp, over and over again; about how he used to tell Joe, even when the lad was too tiny to understand, that Daddy loved him because he was a boy but that women were trash. I told them how Nathan punched me in the stomach that day and how, suddenly, I knew I couldn't stay. I even told them how I never bonded with Joe.

They were nice. They never said one word in criticism. They just listened, even when I broke down and cried.

I was on the point of telling them about the letter that Jarvis wrote to me that day, the one telling me that if only I would go to him, he would love and cherish me forever, when a police officer tapped on the door and asked if he could have an urgent word with the inspector. They were only gone a moment and when he came back I could tell he had some news.

'We've just had a phone call from a woman in Eddington, Sussex,' he said. 'Her dog found . . . '

He hesitated for just a second. I gripped the edge of the table. Awful images swept through my mind.

'. . . a silver trainer at the edge of a track when they were out walking,' he finished.

'Is it Katie's?'

He sighed deeply.

'We don't know for sure,' he muttered. 'The dog brought it back to the woman and she threw it away. It wasn't until she got home and saw the lunch time news bulletin that things began to click. But from her description, it sounds pretty much like it. Yes.'

I could feel my breath coming in shorter and shorter bursts. My lips began to tingle and I felt light-headed.

'Does that mean ... ?'

I couldn't verbalise my worst thoughts. If Katie had lost a shoe, what other clothing had she lost? Had someone ... ?

'Sussex police are still questioning the woman,' the detective explained. 'She remembers seeing a Land Rover with what she called "a couple of kids" in it. She says they were fooling around – she didn't think much of it because it was farmland and you don't need a licence to drive.'

He paused.

'She did say that as the jeep drove off she heard someone scream,' he added. 'Sadly, she's the type to mind her own business – her words, not mine – so that was that.'

Suddenly it was all too much. I felt as if I was watching a fast-moving video: Katie as a baby being thrown into the air by Jarvis and giggling for all she was worth; Katie starting school in her brown and gold uniform and her hair in bunches; Katie learning to ride a bike.

And worse.

I saw myself hitting her, pushing her down the stairs, vomiting in the mornings while she sobbed outside the bathroom door. I remembered the way she would stand by my bed in the early hours of the morning when the nightmares made me wake up screaming and how I would turn and see those big eyes and think, just for an instant, that it was little Joseph.

196

And because it wasn't, I would take all my guilt out on Katie.

'I've been such a bad mother, Inspector!' I sobbed. 'But just find my Katie, and I swear I'll be good. Please, please, find her, please...'

He called a woman detective in then and they brought me yet another cup of tea. They've said I can go home in a bit.

I don't know if I want to.

I don't think I can face being on my own, just waiting.

'Lydia!' The door bursts open and the inspector is back, and this time he is smiling.

'Katie's made contact!'

What? What did he say? I stare at him. I thought he said Katie...

'She tried to call us,' he said. 'She was in distress, but we've traced the signal and narrowed down our search. We've deployed every available police car in the area; we've got tracker dogs and a police helicopter scanning the countryside. We'll find her, Lydia. We will!'

It's odd.

I can nod at him but I can't speak. I open my mouth but no sound comes out. All I can do is pray.

'I don't suppose...'

The inspector hesitates.

'What?'

'Well, Katie said something about Foxhill or Fox...'

'Foxhole! Oh my God, he's taken her to Foxhole Farm!'

The inspector is all attention now.

'You know it?'

I nod.

'It's in Sussex – you know that – it's a really tumbledown place, not far from Fulking – I can't remember the name of the road...'

'Right! That's brilliant!'

And he's gone leaving me with yet another constable.

All I can do now is keep praying. Dear God, I've been bad, I've sinned, I've made a million mistakes but if You bring Katie back to me I'll do anything, whatever it takes. Anything.

'Are you all right, Mrs Fordyce?'

I nod at the constable and just keep on praying.

TOM
Monday July 2nd
5.15 p.m.

I won't look at them. Not at the teacher, not at the dinner, not at the video.

You can't look at anything when the back-of-the-head pain comes and it's coming now. Hot, spiky, crawling up my neck and into my head and making my legs kick and my arms wave.

Hit the head, hit the pain, make it go away.

Close my eyes, press my hands into them, so that orange and purple and green flashes dance and make patterns.

Katie's there. Katie's in the patterns. Katie calling, Katie crying.

Katie's in the orange flashes.

'KATIE! KATIE!'

Teacher's running, taking my hands, pulling them away from my eyes.

Kick her.

Make her go.

I want the patterns. I want the flashes.

I want to see Katie.

KATIE
Monday July 2nd
5.20 p.m.

He's going mad. He's lighting matches and throwing them round the room. The flapping end of a curtain catches fire and flares; he lights the other one. Flames lick upwards.

He lights a candle and hurls it into the pile of newspapers. The corners catch and curl; thin wisps of smoke spiral upwards.

Now he's beside me, lighted match in hand.

'No, Joe, no!'

But he grabs my hand and drags me, pulls me to my feet. I scream as the pain in my ribs makes me fall forward, gripping my chest.

He drags me to the window. The curtain has burnt, the flames are spreading along the frilly pelmet to the other side. He lights matches and hurls them outside; the towering weeds, dry from the summer sun, kindle, catch in the breeze and begin licking their way along the side of the house.

He swings round and stares at me.

'Take your clothes off!'

I won't. I can't. I back away.

'You have to do it! I don't want you to die!'

I stop. Stare at him, heart pounding, mouth dry as the smell of smoke begins to filter through my nostrils.

'I'll burn your clothes and he'll think you're dead!'

He pushes me against the wall, drops down onto one knee and struggles with my one remaining shoe.

I lift my foot and kick him hard in the one place where I know men hurt most.

He cries out and rolls onto one side, clutching his crotch.

'You stupid, stupid . . .' His sobs muffle his words.

I run to the door. The dry grass is burning but the flames haven't reached the path. Stones cut into my feet as I run, and my lungs feel as if they will burst as the pain in my ribs gets worse with every step.

I can hear the crackle of flames behind me. I glance over my shoulder and stop.

Joe isn't chasing me.

Joe is still inside.

'Joe!'

I turn and scream, but as I take in breath the pain is too much; I fall forward, face down into stinging nettles.

Why doesn't he come out? He'll die if he stays in there.

I struggle to my feet, my cheeks burning from the nettles, my eyes watering as the smoke from the house wafts towards me.

I can't just leave him.

But why not? He was the one who kept leaving me, tied me up, hit me. He was the one who planned to leave me to die in those flames.

Only he couldn't do it. When it came to it, he didn't want me to die. He said so.

And I don't want him to die.

He's my brother.

I take a step back towards the house but I can't do it. I can't go back. I can't take the risk.

I have to get help. Maybe, if I could just get back up to the main track, I'll see someone. A farmer, a hiker – someone.

I can't run any more. I can only walk and even that hurts. I wrap my arms round my chest and stumble on, my eyes scanning right and left, praying that someone will come.

I have to stop. I feel so sick, my head is spinning. I have to sit down, just for a minute. A minute won't matter.

I force myself to look back at the house. The smoke is billowing out of the window.

Joe will die.

I can't wait. I have to move.

Tears stream down my face. My head throbs, my ears buzz.

The buzzing gets louder.

I wish it would stop. All I want to do is lie down and sleep.

But it doesn't stop, it gets louder – an incessant whirring like an engine.

An engine!

I look up and there it is. A helicopter, flying over the house and towards me.

I jump to my feet, waving my arms, shouting, crying.

An arm comes out. Someone waves back.

'Joe's in there!' I scream but of course, they won't hear.

The helicopter hovers, then suddenly spins round and moves away.

'Don't leave me!'

They can't go. I know they'll get help but I can't cope any more. The pain's so bad, my legs feel numb, my eyes are blurring and I'm so so scared. I want someone here with me. Now.

But it's not going – it's hovering near the track, just above the hedge. Suddenly, above the whirring of the rotor blades, I hear a siren. My heart almost stops; I don't dare look. Please, please let it be.

It's coming nearer. I turn my head.

A police car screeches to a halt, doors slam, two figures run, then pause.

'Here! I'm here!'

A whistle blows and they're running towards me.

It's OK now.

Now I can sit down and sleep.

LYDIA
Monday July 2nd
6.10 p.m.

They've found her! They've found my Katie! She's hurt and she's in shock but she's alive!

They're taking her to hospital in Brighton and they're sending a car for me so that I can get down there and be with her.

They found Joseph too but they said they would tell me about him once we were on our way. Tom's teacher has said she'll have him at the school till I get back; it's a good thing they've a few spare residential beds. I don't know how he'll cope with sleeping over, because he hates unfamiliar places, but what can I do? They say Katie may have to be in hospital for a couple of days and right now, that's where I have to be.

I must let Grace know that Katie's safe. It'll be odd going back to Brighton; the day I left, I vowed I'd never go back again.

Now I can't wait to get there.

KATIE
Monday July 2nd
8.00 p.m.

They won't tell me anything about Joe. Does that mean he's dead? All they say is that I must rest and stop worrying. They've given me two white pills and said that everything will be just fine.

But it's not fine for Joe. He scares me and I don't ever want to be alone with him ever again but I don't want him to die. In the end, he saved me; he could have killed me, his dad

203

wanted me dead but Joe couldn't do it.

I feel so tired but I can't stop thinking about him, lying on the floor with the fire taking hold. If I hadn't kicked him the way I did, he wouldn't have fallen, and if he hadn't fallen...

If he dies, it will be because of me. He let me live and I've killed him.

'Now, now, Katie love, what's all this?'

The ward sister perches herself on the end of my bed even though there's a notice forbidding anyone to do such a terrible thing. I realise that I'm crying out loud.

'Is Joe alive? You have to tell me? Is he? Is he?'

'Joe?'

She looks puzzled.

'The boy in the house...with the fire...my brother...'

My eyelids are drooping.

'You just sleep, sweetheart,' she says soothingly. 'And when you wake up your mum will be here. That'll be nice, won't it?'

Nice. Yes. Mum. But what about Joe?

'Joe? How's Joe?'

The figure of the nurse is swimming and blurring in front of my eyes.

'I'll find out – you just think about dropping off to sleep, there's a good girl.'

Think about sleep. Think about Joe later.

Sleep now. So tired. So so tired.

TOM
Monday July 2nd
8.30 p.m.

My teacher's gone and left me here with the fat lady they call Matron. I don't want to go to bed here: I want my bed with the swirly cover and the lumpy bit by my feet.

Matron Lady says that I have to sleep here because Mum has gone to get Katie. She says it's because I've been a very good boy and drawn so nicely that they've found Katie.

Katie went away to the place with animals and foxes. She went with the Joe man. I want Mum to bring Katie back but I don't want the Joe man.

He's bad.

I know he is.

I'm not stupid.

GRACE
Monday July 2nd
10.00 p.m.

I don't know why I keep staring at the telephone. It's not as if the first thing Lyddy is going to do when she gets to the hospital is phone me, is it? Bill says I should just be thankful that the poor child is alive and in hospital, but I keep asking myself how she must be feeling? What's happened to her these last few days? You hear such dreadful things on the news; it makes my stomach churn just thinking about it.

And then there's the question of Lydia and this Joseph boy. If she really is his mother, what's going to happen now? And if she did marry poor Jarvis while she still had a husband, will she get punished?

She should be there by now.

I can just imagine how she'll feel when she sees Katie. I know how I'd feel if Gareth walked through the front door right now.

He won't, of course. Bill says I spend far too much time in wishful thinking.

Sometimes wishful thinking is all you've got.

LYDIA
Monday July 2nd
11.45 p.m.

I can't take my eyes off her. She's sleeping now, her poor little face a mass of bruises and her collar bone broken. The doctor told me she has two cracked ribs and a mass of cuts on her feet, but otherwise she's unharmed. Thank God.

The nurses keep trying to persuade me to go and get some sleep, but I can't move. I still feel that if I turn my back for a second, she'll vanish again.

When I first saw her, I couldn't speak. I just wrapped her in my arms and held her and rocked her and we both cried. They were ever so good, the nurses; they pulled the curtains round her bed, and left us in peace for a bit.

Then suddenly Katie and I were talking at the same time, falling over our words in order to get our thoughts out.

'Mum, I'm sorry, I'm so sorry!'

'Katie, forgive me! I didn't mean . . . '

'Mum, it was Joseph and he said . . . '

'Katie, it's OK. I know. I'll tell you everything when . . . '

'Mum, is he dead? Is he, Mum? You have to tell me.'

That brought me up short.

'Dead? No, darling, he's not dead but don't you worry, I'll never let him get near you again and . . . '

Katie grabbed my hand.

'He's not dead? You promise? He's really alive?'

She seemed happy. I couldn't work it out.

'He's been taken to another hospital,' I told her. 'Smoke inhalation and a few burns. Nothing he doesn't richly deserve. When I think of what he tried to do . . . '

206

I choked. I couldn't go on. Even then, seeing Katie alive and well, the thought of what might have happened was too horrifying to contemplate.

'He could have killed me, Mum,' Katie blurted out. 'But he didn't. When it came to it, he couldn't do it, even though his dad . . . '

I could see her hesitate.

'He was my father, too, wasn't he?' she whispered.

For an instant, I wanted to deny it, tell her that she'd got it all wrong, but I've done with lies and pretence. I made a promise to God and I will keep it.

'Yes,' I whispered. 'But it was Jarvis that loved you, Jarvis that thought of you as his very own. He never found out, you know . . . '

'He did, Mum! That's why he killed himself, because Nathan kept blackmailing him and he couldn't carry on any longer.'

My blood froze in my veins.

'Nathan? But how . . . ?'

'He kept tracks on us both, Mum, all those years!' She gave an involuntary shudder. 'He knew that I was his daughter because of my eyes.'

Those eyes held my gaze and it was me who looked away first.

'He threatened all sorts of things and Dad paid him to keep away and keep quiet,' Katie whispered, clearly conscious of the patient in the next bed. 'And in the end, Dad just ran out of money.'

For a while, we didn't speak. We just sat there, crying and holding hands. I thought about Jarvis and how he always wanted the best for all of us, how he never turned down overtime, and how he hated to waste money. I remembered the betting shop tickets and how angry I'd been, shouting at him long after the funeral and asking why he had to gamble when he wouldn't let me have a new kitchen.

I knew what Katie's next question would be long before she asked it.

'Mum, why did you leave? Why didn't you take Joe with you?'

The first part of the question was easy to answer. I told her about the beatings and I guess, because of what the poor kid had been through with Joseph, she could identify with what it was like.

'And Joe?' she persisted.

I could have told her anything, I guess. I could have pretended that I meant to go back for Joe when I got settled, constructed some story about wanting to leave something behind for Nathan. But I promised God there would be no more lies.

'I . . . I never loved him.'

The words were out. They sounded harsh and brutal, but they were the truth and for me, that was one giant step forward.

'I didn't know how, Katie,' I whispered and I didn't care that the tears were welling up in my eyes. 'I'm not trying to shift the blame, but no one ever loved me as a kid – except Grace, of course. My dad shoved me into a children's home and when I did go back to him at the age of sixteen, he either ignored me or lashed out at me. So I ran to the first man who liked me.'

'Nathan?' Katie was watching my face intently.

I nodded.

'Odd, isn't it? I ran away from a brutal uncaring father straight into the arms of a brutal uncaring man,' I mused. 'When I found I was pregnant with Joseph, Nathan was furious. He didn't want a kid, he said; and he made it quite clear that if he felt marginalised by a baby, I'd be for it.'

'So you tried not to love Joe?'

I shrugged.

'I didn't have to try,' I admitted. 'After he was born I had post natal depression – really badly. I couldn't eat, sleep – couldn't even be bothered to change the baby's nappy. And the odd thing was that Nathan took over; it was as if, even when Joseph was a tiny mite, they ganged up on me.'

I sighed.

'I used to hear him upstairs talking to Joseph in his cot, saying what a waste of space his mother was. I guess he's been doing that ever since.'

I squeezed Katie's hand.

'And after everything that has happened lately, you probably feel that too.'

Katie flung her arms round my neck.

'I don't, Mum,' she said. 'I hate it when you go ballistic but I love you. I really do.'

Her eyes filled with tears.

'Do you . . . I mean, do you get cross because you don't know how to love me?'

That question almost broke my heart. I couldn't blame her for asking; not after the way I'd behaved.

'Katie, I love you so much,' I told her, wrapping her in my arms. 'All these years, I've felt so guilty.'

I cried some more then, but Katie hadn't quite finished.

'What about the baby who died?'

I swallowed hard.

'There wasn't one,' I confessed. 'I told you that because I worried that one day I might be in hospital or something and you'd see on my notes that I'd had three children, not two. I didn't want you searching for . . .'

The words stuck in my throat.

'. . . for your brother.'

Katie looked as if she had a load more questions she wanted to ask, but just then, the nurse came back, all firm and dictatorial and told me that Katie needed to rest. She fell asleep holding my hand. She's still holding it and I won't let go.

I won't ever let go of her again.

KATIE
Wednesday July 4th
1 p.m.

I know it's silly but the nearer we get to home, the more shaky I feel. It's not that I wanted to stay in hospital; I couldn't wait to get out of the place. It's just that while I was on the ward, all the awful things that had happened to me over the last few days seemed like a bad dream, something I could put in a box and forget about.

I can't forget, though. I don't think I ever will.

We're almost there. We've just passed Spectacle Lane, past the very tree under which I met Joe for the first time. If Mum and I hadn't argued that morning, if I hadn't run off in the rain, none of this would ever have happened. My life would just have gone on as before.

Except that I know that's not true. Joe was determined to find me and in the end, he would have done. In a way, I'm glad he did because now there can be no more pretending between Mum and me. I don't have to go through every week trying not to make her cross, because it was never really me that made her cross in the first place. She was cross with herself, haunted by the past and trying all the time to run away from it.

We've had loads of talks and she's treating me like a proper adult. I guess it won't last; there'll be more arguments and I'll flip and shout back, but at least it won't be like before. She's promised to get some help with her drinking and her mood swings and I think she really means it, because I overheard her asking the ward sister for some leaflets before we left. She says that she's scared, because she reckons counselling will be really painful and I'm scared too. I've decided I have to talk to someone about Joe. Joe and me.

I wish I could really hate him, put him right out of my mind and never give him another thought as long as I live, but I can't. I don't love him – or at least, I don't think I do. It's just that I keep thinking about the way he was at the end, lost, confused and – oh, I don't know – looking for love, I guess.

I guess we all look for love, every single day. What I'm worried about is that there's no one there for Joe. The police told me that Nathan is psychotic. I'm not sure what that means but one of the sergeants said it was all proof that care in the community wasn't working and if they had anything to say, he'd be back in a psychiatric hospital pretty quickly. It's no wonder Joe's a mess, and I reckon Mum and I have to do something to help.

I tried to say that but now is not the time. Maybe in a few days...

My stomach's going over. We're turning into Church Hill and I can see the house. The police driver who brought us back is opening the car door, murmuring something to Mum about letting us have some time alone before more questions.

'Come on, Pumpkin!' Mum's key is in the lock. The door swings open.

'Katie, Katie, welcome home!'

Grace is there, and Mrs Ostler with Tom. There's a huge cake with yellow icing on the table and the room seems to be full of flowers. Grace is hugging me, smelling of jasmine and gingerbread, tears running down her cheeks.

Tom is watching me. I've missed him so much. How can that be? He drives me crazy half the time and yet now all I want to do is talk to him.

'Tom? I'm back, Tom?'

I want to hug him but you don't do that with Tom, not till he shows he's ready.

'Are you OK, Tom?'

Tom is staring at me. He takes a step towards me.

His face puckers in a frown.

'Kayhee.'

In the room nothing moves. No one breathes. Time stands still.

'Kayhee home!'

After ten years and five months, Tom has said something.

Suddenly, we're all laughing and crying and trying desperately not to hug him and make him upset.

Tom looks at us, and then turns and walks away. Within seconds he is rocking quietly in the corner.

We're not part of his world any more, not at this moment, but I know – I just know – that we will be again.

I'm so proud of him. He's my brother. My younger brother. I have two, you know.

More Fiction for you to enjoy

The FIRING

by Richard MacSween

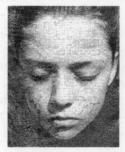

Stuck in a poxy village where nothing happens
Anna has to ask herself what she's done wrong?
Having to share living space with a useless
stepfather. And don't even mention those twins.

Things can only get better when a stranger arrives.
Two strangers – there's a son as well. And his stupid
name is only the first mystery about him.

**'A cracking first novel – sharp, funny and
authentic yet haunted by the strange magic
of a fairy tale. Anna is a teenage heroine for
our time.'** Blake Morrison

'An exceptional first novel.' Melvin Burgess

ISBN 1842700553 £4.99

More Fiction for you to enjoy

WiNGS TO FLY

by

PATRICK COOPER

I couldn't stop thinking about the Birdman, and that story he'd told me. It got mixed up inside me with the talk of the war and my mother's crying, and I had nightmares of screaming aeroplanes and charred hands and black, broken faces.

Sarah was thirteen when she met Julian, the Birdman. He told her about the Great War – about flying and fighting in the skies over France, about being wounded, and the death of his friend Harry. She was strangely drawn to him in this time of tumultuous change, a time of danger and loss, a time of growing up and of finding the wings to fly . . .

'A subtly poignant book' *achuka.co.uk*

'A moving story of love, loss and the devastating effects of war' *Financial Times*

ISBN 184270026X £4.99

More Fiction for you to enjoy

RIVER of SECRETS
by Griselda Gifford

Fran is very upset because her mother has remarried
and she has to live with her stepfather and his son
at her gran's old home. She was very fond of her
gran, who has recently been found dead in the
nearby river. Was her death an accident? Fran is
sure someone is to blame and she's determined to
solve the mystery. Is the weird girl, Fay, who lives
next door, hiding something? And why does
another new friend, Denny, warn her against Fay's
strange magic? Fran faces danger when the river
almost claims a new victim, before she finally
unlocks its secrets in a surprising and exciting
climax to the story.

'A nail-biting novel' 4 star review, *Mizz Magazine*

ISBN 1842700456 £4.99

More Fiction for you to enjoy

LADY

MY LIFE AS A BITCH

by Melvin Burgess

Sandra Francy is 17 and having too much fun.
Everyone wants to stop her but the problem is, she
likes it. When she gets accidentally turned into a
dog she's horrified at first but soon starts to wonder
if being human is worth the effort. Her attempts to
hang on to her humanity are bizarre and often
hilarious – but her life as a dog leads her to
pleasures she hardly knew existed.

'**Very powerfully written**' John Carey, Newsnight

'**Succeeds in summing up the feelings of a
generation**' Jack Landesman, 15, *Sunday Times*

ISBN 0862647703 £10.99 (hbk)